HOW TO ROPE A VALIANT COWBOY

SILVER SPRINGS RANCH: BOOK 5

ANYA SUMMERS

D1517603

Published by S & G Books LLC
P.O. Box 3353
Ballwin, Missouri 63022
USA

How To Rope A Valiant Cowboy
Anya Summers

Image By: R+M Photography

Cover Model: Scott Holliday

Print ISBN 979-8-5321507-4-4

Ebook ISBN 978-1-7370605-1-2

ABOUT THE BOOK

Retired Navy Seal Duncan has a stellar set up. After years of covert operations dodging bullets, he's living the high life, teaching tourists basic outdoor survival skills at Silver Springs Ranch. The only thing he is evading these days are the countless women trying to trap him into a relationship. He enjoys women and their company immensely, but the institute of marriage and committed relationships are not for him.

And yet the newest maid, Eve, leaves him stymied. She's heart-stoppingly gorgeous, one of the worst maids he has ever encountered, and is holding on to dark secrets—ones that engage his every need to protect and shield her from whatever darkness eats at her.

She's a total thorn in his side, turning him inside out and tying him up in knots with unquenchable desire. Due to the severity of his fascination, he cuts a wide berth around her, figuring it's best to stay as far away from her as possible...

Until she comes to him one night and begs him to teach her self-defense. Duncan discovers he can't contain his need any longer, not when she is looking to him for guidance—and like his every fantasy come to life. He yearns to have her on her knees, begging for his dominance.

And when she becomes a target, he will do whatever it takes to save her.

PROLOGUE

With her arms loaded with groceries, Kate headed in through the door between the house and four-car garage. It was Friday night, the week before Thanksgiving. Most of her girlfriends were meeting at their favorite bar for happy hour in downtown Savannah, but her only plans tonight were stress baking while drinking a bottle of Pinot Grigio. Rather pathetic for a twenty-eight-year-old single woman, but she couldn't seem to focus on her lack of a love life with work being so crazy here lately. Nor did she have the energy for self-pity over the sad, lonely state of her life.

It had been one hell of a week at the bank. The thought of socializing any further this week made Kate grimace. She'd rather go get parts of her anatomy waxed than have to deal with people. In fact, she would have to be dynamited out of the house this weekend to get her to leave before Monday morning.

Owning a bank came with a metric ton of drama, more than most people realized. And when it was a career that you never intended to pursue but performed out of love for people who were no longer alive, the theatrics were infinitely more stressful. If Kate was honest with herself, the constant strain left little happiness in her daily life. She slogged through her days by telling herself each morning that her parents would be proud she had carried on the family tradition. Even though the thought was cold comfort.

It was why she turned to her love of baking so often. It soothed her soul in ways nothing else did.

Maybe she should accept the corporate buyer's offer. If she sold Jefferson Bank and Trust, the small town chain of banks begun by her great grandfather, then she could remove the stress overload from her life. The substantial offer was more than enough money, and would last her a few lifetimes. With the money they were offering, Kate wouldn't need to work another day in her life.

She could take a vacation. Rent a seaside bungalow on a tropical island, and just relax for a change of pace. She could go back to the culinary institute and finish up her studies. The world would be her oyster. She could do something, anything, to shake herself out of the constant malaise that hovered around her.

Since the moment Kate had inherited the company six years ago from her deceased parents at the ripe age of twenty-two, she had been approached by buyers multiple times.

But thus far, she hadn't been able to let it go. Not when it was all she had left of her father, and their family.

Sighing, she nudged the door with her shoulder and

pushed her way inside the only home she had ever known. The stately colonial had been in the family for three generations. Other than her stint in college for her business degree and her one semester at the culinary institute, she had never lived anywhere else. Why would she, with a house that was paid off? All she had to contend with was the upkeep.

Kate figured that one day, her kid would reside in the same bedroom she had grown up in. Granted, she would have to find a guy first, and those were in short supply because she didn't trust her judgment when it came to men.

Carting bags chock-full of baking supplies into the spotless kitchen with its professional grade, stainless steel appliances, Kate dumped her purchases on the ivory granite countertop. She figured she would crack open the wine first, perhaps nibble on some cheese and prosciutto while she made zucchini bread—which to her mind, constituted getting her veggies in for today. She shifted, and gripped the red leather strap to lift the crossbody purse off her body.

"Hello, Kate." A distinct, unforgettable, gritty male voice disturbed the silence. It was the voice of a man who smoked two packs of cigarettes daily for decades, the sound like sandpaper scraping over concrete.

Thick, suffocating fear enveloped her. It constricted her chest painfully as panic set in and sent her heart racing.

How was *he* here?

Dread infused her as she defensively swiveled in the direction of the resonant tones that ripped apart the silence. That deep, male baritone was a voice from her past. One that Kate had never thought she would hear again. Clenching her hand around her keys, she fought the bile rising up in her throat as her gaze landed on him.

The smug bastard was smirking, the corners of his thin lips curled up. But the smile didn't reach his eyes. He had cold eyes. Dead eyes. Eyes that reminded her of a cobra seconds before it struck a killing blow. He couldn't be here. He was supposed to be serving twenty years in the state penitentiary system.

She had to be hallucinating that Trevor was standing in her kitchen wearing jeans and a black shirt. His bald scalp reflected the overhead light, which only served to make his blunt facial features even harsher.

"What are you doing here?" She was proud her voice remained steady when she spoke and didn't relay her fright even for a moment.

"Did you really think we wouldn't come? You betrayed us."

"Your brother is here too?" She glanced around, never letting her gaze stray too far from the violent, dangerous man before her. His brother, Silas, was the last man on Earth she ever wanted to cross paths with again.

They weren't the ones who had been betrayed four years ago. Silas and his brother Trevor had cruelly deceived Kate. They had used her, only to try and take everything from her by force. They were the reason she had trust issues when it came to men. They had played her for a fool. Silas had broken her heart and left her wondering if she could ever trust her own judgement when it came to men.

"Sadly, no. Silas died in prison a year ago. And for that, you will pay." Trevor sneered, slowly sauntering her way with sadistic, fanatical glee blazing in his gaze.

Her heart stopped.

It was then she understood that he planned to kill her, and would enjoy doing it. She knew that truth as it resonated deep in the marrow of her bones. In his warped mind, he had already handed down a conviction—blaming her for his transgressions and the consequences that followed.

Spying the gun tucked into his pants, Kate retreated. She took a step back and then another, with an eye toward placing the kitchen island between them before she escaped. Wracking her brain, she tried to figure a way out of this situation that wouldn't result in her death.

The menacing glare in Trevor's eyes stated plainly that he had every intention of killing her. It wouldn't be quick, either. He would make it painful. The bastard would enjoy her screams. She could bet that by the time he was finished, she'd welcome death like a long lost lover instead of the great leveler of humanity.

Everything inside her rebelled at the thought of surrendering.

Keep him talking. It was all she could think of, given Trevor had always been a boastful ass. "It's not my fault Silas died. You and your brother used me to get to Jefferson Bank and Trust, to steal from me and the bank patrons."

"Once we had the intel on the bank, I told my brother to get rid of you, said that you were a liability we didn't need, and I was right. We went to prison because of you."

The dude was crazy and had been feeding himself a pack of lies, acting as if he was the victim when the reverse was true. "No. You went to prison because you robbed my family's bank at gunpoint and shot the guard on duty, who is in a wheelchair for life because of you."

"Come now, Kate, it was your testimony that put us away. Without it, and the story you sang for the jury, my brother and I would have walked."

"The two of you made your choices the moment you decided to commit armed robbery." She inched her way toward the door as he neared. If she could just make it to her car, she would survive.

"My brother trusted you, loved you—"

"Using someone isn't love." Silas had used Kate's feelings for him against her when it counted. For that, she couldn't forgive him, not even in death. May he rot in everlasting hell.

Hope surged as she neared the door to the garage. Only three feet left. She could do this—escape him, and find help.

Trevor rushed her, grabbing her with his large, strong hands. With startling ease, he slammed her up against the adjoining wall. Pain ricocheted throughout her body as the impact thud echoed in the kitchen. He had only been toying with her, like a cat playing with a mouse before it struck the killing blow.

Before she could regain her footing, his hands firmly circled her neck. With triumphant glee filling his dark gaze, he squeezed. Those thick, tough fingers cut off her air supply. Gasping for breath, she fought against his hold, trying to pry his hands off. But she was like a fly trying to bat away a tiger. Black spots swam in her field of vision. She was seconds from passing out.

Trevor leaned in close enough that his, hot foul breath that smelled like an ashtray washed over her face. "How does it feel, bitch, knowing that you damned yourself when you helped send us to prison?"

She was still clutching the keys. Gripping them tightly, with the keys poking out between her fingers, with the last ounce of strength she possessed, she punched her fist up and forward as hard and as fast as she could before she lost consciousness. Her fist connected with his left eye. Blood spurted in a warm, metallic spray.

Trevor roared in agony.

One minute, she couldn't breathe. The next, she was slumped against the wall, gulping in air. Blood poured down Trevor's face and dripped from his hands covering his wounded eye. Blood was splattered over her tile floor, on her blouse, on her fingers, and likely elsewhere.

This was her chance to escape while he danced around in anguish.

Not wasting another second, she yanked open the door to the garage and rushed to her car, glad that she hadn't taken her purse off.

Jesus Christ! She'd taken out his eye. She wanted to vomit. She wanted to give in to the urge to scream, but once she started, she would likely never stop.

But most of all, she wanted to live.

She hit the garage door button on her way out. Thankfully, she hadn't locked the car. Heaving the driver side door open, she bolted inside. Once inside, she hit the car locks then shoved the bloody key into the ignition and turned it. The engine revved to life.

Trevor stood in the doorway. He was holding a towel over his eye, his free hand clenched. With fear and self-preservation guiding her actions, Kate threw the Mercedes into reverse.

"I'll find you. No matter where you go. I will find you and end you, bitch!" he hollered with rage contorting his bloody features.

She slammed on the gas before he could close the garage door, then reversed out of the garage and down her driveway at speeds that would make a race car driver proud. Barely stopping the car to throw it into drive, she sped away, glancing in her rearview mirror every three seconds to see if he'd followed her.

What should she do? Go to the police? But how could they help her?

She had to at least file a report, let them know what happened. She doubted it would keep her safe. Prison had made him crazy, with a single-minded goal: killing her.

Trevor would come for her again. Kate understood that fact down to the marrow of her bones. She didn't know how he'd gotten out of prison already when he was supposed to be serving twenty years. The only thing she did know, was that he would make good on his threat. If tonight was anything to go by, he wouldn't rest until she was dead.

And that was why she had to bury Kate Jefferson before the night was through.

1

_____

One year later

$\mathcal{A}$ midst rolling meadows and slate peaks, the log cabin style hotel stood like a welcoming beacon, beckoning Eve with a glimmer of hope that this was a place where she could hide, and no one would discover that she used to be Kate. That here, amidst the jagged, snowcapped mountains and evergreen valleys, the pastures teaming with steer and horses, she could stop running. In all her days, she had never seen the sky so achingly blue. Maybe it was the difference in elevation. Or the fact that the air wasn't clogged with fossil fuels and pollution that made it so ripe a blue that seemed to stretch on forever.

She glanced at the newspaper advertisement in her hand, and the name she had written beside it when she'd made the call from the payphone at the diner in Denver.

Silver Springs Ranch was a working dude ranch and was run by a woman, Amber Anderson. Surely that would work in Eve's favor.

Except, what if she didn't get the job? Where would she go then?

She hadn't the foggiest clue.

All she had done for the last year was run. Her financial situation was precarious. She couldn't remember the last time she had slept soundly for a full eight hours without the ever-present fear that Trevor would find her again dogging her every thought and movement.

Drawing up the last reserves of her strength, she exited her truck. Hiding the nerves making her hands tremble, she clutched her purse. Her breath plumed in white puffs as an icy wind—carrying the scent of snow with it—swirled around her as she approached the rustic lodge. The building was a good three stories tall, a blend of hickory-colored wood logs and shimmering, clear glass that gleamed in the sunlight. There was a wide veranda with plenty of pewter Adirondack chairs for guests to relax in and watch all the activity on the ranch.

On her short trek through the parking lot, the cold sank beneath the threadbare tan coat she had picked up at a second-hand shop, and she shivered. She shoved her hands in the coat pockets. She didn't particularly care for the cold. Never really had. However, she would make an exception if it meant she could completely disappear and never have Trevor find her again.

Enticing, toe-curling pleasurable heat encircled her as she pushed her way inside through the red front doors, and ambled into the hotel lobby.

Inside, it was charming, with rustic, Western style décor. It was part rustic elegance, part garish display with the mounted animal heads hung up on the walls. In the lobby seating area was a stuffed black bear standing on its hindlegs amidst comfortable couches, and a baby grand piano sat in the opposite corner near the entrances to the ballroom.

With Christmas only seven weeks away, the lobby had been turned into a festive wonderland, with garlands and tinsel strung up on every immobile surface. Even the bear had been decorated with a Santa hat and red scarf. Enormous tall pine Christmas trees that were fully lit added their spicy scent to the air. The fireplace in the lobby roared with a cheery fire. It was homey. It made a person want to curl up by the fireplace with a cup of hot cocoa and admire the view out the windows.

Hotel guests stood near the entrance to a restaurant with engaging aromas wafting in from the open arched doorway. From what Eve could see past the hostess stand, it had been designed with down home comfort in mind, and the Christmas decorations had taken over that place too. Her mouth watered at the delicious smells. Over the past year, she had skipped so many meals, her clothes hung loose. And the breakfast sandwich she had indulged in this morning while filling her car had not lasted. It was already midafternoon, and she was starving.

Sadly, she turned away from the restaurant and headed in the opposite direction to the reservation desk. Interview first, and then she could get something to eat. If she got the job, she would indulge in a meal here at the hotel restaurant.

A lovely blonde, with long hair that spilled over her shoulders and who was dressed in a smart navy blazer and slacks, stood behind the counter. She cast Eve a beaming smile as she approached the desk. "Welcome to Silver Springs Ranch. Do you have a reservation?"

"No. I have an interview with Amber Anderson. She told me to ask for her at the reservation desk." Eve tried not to fidget as the woman's gaze shifted and assessed her.

"Oh, all right. And your name?"

"Eve Carruthers." She glanced at the clerk's nametag. The blonde's name was Jessica. They didn't have the last name or even the first initial of the last name on their badges.

"I'll let her know you are here." Jessica smiled pleasantly and picked up the receiver on the desk phone. "Hi Amber, it's Jessica. I have an Eve Carruthers here to see you for an interview... Uh huh, sure, I can do that." Then she hung up after saying, "Be there in just a few minutes."

"She's ready for you now. Please follow me. I will escort you to her office. Mike, I'll be back in five minutes. Need me to bring you back anything?" Jessica asked her coworker behind the desk.

"I'm good. But thanks." The older gentleman with salt and pepper hair nodded with a grin, then directed his attention toward another guest.

"Right this way." Jessica stepped out from behind the counter and gestured toward the hall on the left. She was a few inches taller than Eve—not that that was hard to do, given she barely cleared five foot even.

"How long have you worked at Silver Springs

Ranch?" Eve asked as they boarded the elevator around the corner from the reservation desk.

"Oh gosh, a little over four years now. It's a great place to work. The Andersons really take care of their people." Jessica was effusive with her response.

"There's more than one?" Eve hoped like hell she wouldn't end up having a multitude of bosses. And there she went, assuming she would get the job as a maid. That confidence originated from all the years she had spent running the bank. In truth, she was overqualified for a job as a maid but fewer questions were asked when she took low-paying positions. It was a lesson learned the hard way over the past year.

She needed the position here, needed the chance to catch her breath. And this place seemed to be a godsend —somewhere she could do that without Trevor catching a whiff of her whereabouts. How many times had she changed her name and her hair color since she'd gone on the run? Especially when the cops had been no help at all. All they had done was file a report after checking out her house, stated she should contact them if she saw him again, and told her to file a petition with the court for a restraining order because Trevor had been released from prison early for good behavior.

But he had found her.

Which was why she had spent the past year moving all around the country.

"Yes. A little over a year ago, the ranch was run by Amber's brother, Colt. But then Colt met his wife, this big-time scientist, and travels the world with her now.

The ranch is owned by the Anderson family, and has been for generations," Jessica said.

"I see," Eve replied, pondering the implications of working for a family business. It could be a mixed bag. But, given the remote location, they might not dig too much into her background. That was the chance she took every time she was forced to run and find a new place to hide. Because Eve Carruthers didn't exist. If someone dug too deep, they would discover the truth. Although, the thought was rather sweet: a guy giving up his career for his wife.

When the elevator stopped at the second floor, Eve followed Jessica off and down a carpeted hall with office doors marked *accounting, marketing, personnel only...* until they arrived at one all the way at the end. On the door was a small plaque with *Amber Anderson, CEO* printed on it.

Before Eve could prepare herself, Jessica knocked on the door and then opened it when a sweet voice from inside said, "Come in."

Eve swallowed her nerves as Jessica entered and said, "Hey Amber."

She trailed the clerk inside the brightly lit office mainly because she didn't want to look like an idiot waiting out in the hall, wringing her hands. In the past year, she had become a shell of her former self, and she hated it. She straightened her spine and forced a smile onto her face.

"Jessica, thanks for bringing her up. Eve, it's a pleasure to meet you." Amber Anderson came around the stately mahogany desk with her hand outstretched and gave Eve a kind smile as the clerk departed, shutting the office door behind her.

The woman was stunning, with her dark inky hair and storm cloud eyes. She was dressed in an ivory blouse, gray slacks, and a pair of killer red heels. Eve worried that her second-hand black and white checkered dress that didn't fit well was all wrong for the interview. The material hung off her frame, making her look like a peasant by comparison to Amber. Especially when it seemed like a lifetime ago that she herself had worn designer clothing and expensive shoes. There were days when she would give anything to have her life back. For her biggest concern to be whether Brent was dating another of his coworkers and causing a ruckus.

Fighting back her nerves and uncertainty, she shook Amber's hand. "It's nice to meet you as well."

"Would you like anything to drink? Water? Coffee?"

Too nervous to be able to swallow anything and keep it down, Eve shook her head. "I'm fine. Although, I might have to make a stop in your restaurant on my way out, the food smells amazing."

"It tastes even better, I can assure you. The bison chili is one of my favorites this time of year. Have a seat, and we can get started." Amber gestured to a pair of wingback chocolate leather chairs.

Eve sat on the edge of one of the chairs facing the desk, trying not to fidget. She had gotten herself ready for the interview in the bathroom at the gas station in town. Which meant, she likely looked like something the cat had not only dragged in, but had chewed up and then spat out. She despised how desperate her life had become.

Amber took her seat behind the desk with a thoughtful expression, like she recognized how ill-fitting Eve's clothes were but was too decent a person to say anything. "So, tell me, what brings you to Colorado looking for work?"

"I needed a change of scenery," Eve lied with a friendly smile instead of admitting the truth—that her ex-boyfriend's one-eyed brother had hunted her across the country, and she needed a place to lie low for a while to catch her breath. She had gotten better with them, the lies and half-truths she'd told to survive. Now they rolled off her tongue with ease when that hadn't always been the case.

"And where are you from?" Amber asked, folding her hands together on the desk.

"Louisiana. Terrebonne Parrish area." Another lie. She had grown up in Savannah, Georgia. Had lived there her entire life—until a year ago.

"That's quite a difference in scenery. What kind of experience do you have working in hotels and the hospitality industry?"

"Truthfully, none. I've waited a lot of tables, though. And I'm sure many of the skills I developed because of it, would translate over well. Fast, efficient service with a smile."

"Do you have any weight restrictions?"

"I'm sorry?" Weight restrictions? What did that have to do with cleaning rooms and mopping floors?

"Any issues lifting heavy items up to fifty pounds?"

"No, not at all." There were times when, by the end of a double shift at whatever crappy restaurant she found work at in the worst parts of town, her trays had seemed like they weighed that much. But Eve was hale and hearty enough, even with exhaustion battering incessantly at her.

"That's good. Being a maid in our hotel is hard work. You would be required to clean guest rooms, strip the bedding, replace it with fresh linens, and towels. Replace all the amenities. And work in a fast and efficient manner to ensure all guest rooms are spotless. Here at Silver Springs Ranch, we pride ourselves on the cleanliness of our rooms and cabins. Then there's the main lobby and other guest spaces that require daily upkeep. And, depending upon your skill level, we also have guest cabins that require cleaning. The frequency of those depends upon the guest."

"I'm certain I can do the job, Miss Anderson. I'm sure there will be a bit of a learning curve. But I'm confident that I can perform the necessary duties." Eve was proud of herself for making her voice sound strong, instead of pleading.

Amber cocked her head. "Why would you want to work here?"

This time, Eve went with honesty. "Because it comes with room and board as part of the salary. If there was a place for me to live back home, that's where I would be, but there isn't. I realize that might make me seem like a bad bet for you, but I promise that, if I'm offered the job, I will work hard, I will be on time, and I'll fill in whenever needed."

"That's good enough for me. The job is yours if you want it," Amber offered with a grin.

Relief flooded Eve. She was being offered an escape. She didn't hesitate with her response. "I do. Thank you so much. You won't regret hiring me."

"I'm sure I won't. Why don't we get the paperwork out of the way? Then I will show you the cabin that will be yours to live in while you work for us."

"Thank you. I won't let you down."

"I'm counting on that," Amber said, withdrawing forms from a desk drawer.

Eve wanted to dance and howl at the moon over landing the maid's position. It was the best thing that had happened to her in longer than she could remember.

———

LATER THAT NIGHT, after Eve had moved in her meager belongings, she indulged in a bowl of the bison chili from the restaurant at the small dinette table in her cabin while staring out the crystal-clear windows as night settled in. It was pitch dark here without all the city lights.

And quiet. Blessedly so. No honking car horns or sounds of the neighbors fighting.

Out here, no one would be able to sneak up on her because she would hear them approach—unlike all the cities she had tried to disappear in to make a fresh start. Even though she had gone to the police, he'd come after her. And then, at each place she had run to, he had found her, time and time again. She had ditched her car. She had changed her name, her hair color, where she lived... all of it.

She was so damn tired of running. Exhaustion and fear were her constant companions.

Yet here, she might be able to really make a fresh start, free from the terror that had dogged her every step. Here, she could disappear. No one paid attention to hotel maids.

And the cabin was hers to stay and live in. The log cabin was fully furnished in a studio type fashion. The only walled off room was the bathroom. But it was significantly better than the seedy, pay-by-the-week motels with stained carpets and questionable bedding that she'd tried to make a home in over the last year.

At least here, she had a real kitchen with a stove and oven, and a full-sized refrigerator with a freezer. She had a pantry, and was already making plans with her first few paychecks to stockpile canned goods, get frozen veggies to store in the freezer, and meat. She could pick up flour and baking supplies; revisit her love of baking.

Then there was the king bed with its red plaid comforter, the golden pine dinette set, and the comfy umber leather couch. There was a small chest of drawers for her to store more clothes. The walls and floors were a gorgeous, honey-gold pine. She had stored the nine-millimeter handgun she had picked up in Memphis a few months ago when she decided it was better to be prepared than not in the nightstand drawer for easy reach.

The owner had given Eve the weekend to get herself settled before she began her new position Monday morning. Was it a job she truly wanted, picking up after and cleaning up other people's messes? Of course not. But she had learned over the past year just how much she was willing to do to keep the wolf from the door.

That was why she had spent almost four full weeks before she landed in Denver, riding commercial buses around the country in a zigzag fashion. She paid cash for everything: bus tickets, meals, all of it, making sure she left no trail behind her, no proof of her existence.

Because, if he found her again, she would die.

$\mathcal{T}$here was little Duncan enjoyed more than the satisfaction of a job well done.

After depositing the guests from his latest camping trip back at registration, he strode toward the elevator. On his agenda—once he'd filed his report with Amber—he planned to head home, shower, eat, and crack open a beer. In that order too. He'd worry about finding company of the female variety after a night alone in his own bed.

Sampson obediently loped at his side. The three-year-old, ninety-five-pound German Shephard loved spending time outdoors as much as he did. Duncan wouldn't mention to the pup that he was getting a bath tonight too. The damn dog would hide and protest and make it almost impossible to get the chore done. But there was no way in hell he was letting the bugger on his couch smelling like bear scat and fish guts. There was little the knucklehead liked more than rolling around in either.

The pair rounded the corner. It was a route Duncan

frequently took, and he rarely paid attention. His focus was on finishing the job of his week-long camping trip with a report on the tracks he'd found around their camp and on the trails, not what was in front of him.

Which was why he collided into the woman at full speed. A soft gasp erupted from her as she froze stiff solid when he grabbed her biceps to steady them both. Duncan almost lost his footing as water sloshed over the rim of the large mop bucket and doused the lower half of his jeans and boots.

Duncan hadn't seen the woman. If he'd been paying attention instead of focused on the task at hand, he would have skirted around her and her bucket. But then, she was a tiny thing, with birdlike bones and big eyes—amber gold eyes that stared up at him, wide with shock. Her raven, blue-black hair was pulled back into a severe bun. She wore no artifice on her heart-shaped, pale cream face.

"Oh no! Look what you made me do." Panic entered her gold eyes. She fought her way out of his hold.

He released her and held up his hands as she backed away. "Sorry. I wasn't watching where I was going."

"No kidding, Sherlock. I was almost finished here too. You need to watch where you are going... and what is that smell?" Her face scrunched up as she glanced from him to Sampson and back in disgust.

"Bear shit. He likes to roll in it." Duncan shrugged, far too familiar with Sampson's exploits to be mad or offended by them, even if he did smell like shit, quite literally.

"And you bring him in here? Don't you have any

manners?" Eve scolded him with a staunch glare, her lush lips curled down with displeasure.

The little maid had some steel in her backbone, practically spitting fire his way. "When it's warranted. I said I was sorry. I can help you—"

"You and your dog have done enough. If I lose this job because of you..." She trailed off with a glare promising retribution, and started mopping up the mess he had caused.

"Look, lady, I didn't mean to run into you. It was an honest mistake."

She nodded curtly. "Just go."

Grinding his teeth, he stepped out of the puddle of water, and whistled for Sampson to follow. With a curse under his breath, he marched the short distance to the elevator.

"Are you kidding me? You're going to traipse over the part I just finished with your wet, filthy boots?"

Duncan glanced back at the maid, one he had never seen before, clenching her fist, and appearing as if she wanted to take his head off. She was a skinny thing. Probably no more than a buck twenty dripping wet. The shapeless maid's uniform did little for her figure. But the sparks in her eyes were electric.

She was delicate, breakable, much like a spitting, enraged kitten, but underneath the clear disdain marring her features was a gorgeous beauty. Being a bit sadistic, he smirked at her reprimand. He'd spent years with superiors yelling at him and getting in his face if he stepped a toe out of line. She could hiss at him all she wanted but he would never back down. It wasn't in his makeup.

"Yep. I've got business with the owner."

She visibly paled. The fight left her form. And at her response, he didn't feel the normal satisfaction he usually did for yanking someone's chain.

"Figures," she muttered and dismissed him, giving him her back as she ran the mop over the puddle on the floor.

And if he noticed that she had a killer ass—well, he was only a guy.

Shaking his head, he climbed on the elevator with Sampson trotting in beside him. On the second floor, he headed to Amber's office and knocked on the door.

"Come in."

Duncan entered with Sampson at his side. "Amber."

"Jesus Christ, you two smell like something that died. Please tell me you didn't walk through the hotel smelling like this. And why are your jeans wet?"

He winced. Being on a camping trip for days at a time, he couldn't help that after a few days, the basic washing that could be done with water from a nearby stream, no longer sufficed. But then, he had spent too many years out on missions in the Navy with no opportunity to bathe, and it didn't tend to faze him when he couldn't get a shower in. "Yeah, sorry about that. I just wanted to report to you first, before heading home for the day."

"Fine. But why are your legs wet?"

"I ran into a maid I've never seen before on the first floor. She was in the middle of mopping. Water spilled everywhere, including my jeans and boots. Totally my fault, though, and not the maid's. Damn woman almost took my head off."

Amber chuckled and shook her head. "Like you can't handle it, or was all that time you spent as a SEAL wasted on you?"

"I didn't say I couldn't handle her." He'd been in far more sticky situations than earning the ire of one little maid.

"Good. Did you at least apologize to Eve?"

So that was her name: the maid with the big, haunted eyes and stellar ass. "I did, not that she accepted my apology." That irritated him. It had been a simple mistake. The world wasn't going to come to an end because he ran into her and spilled mop water.

"She's new. I think she really needs this job. Be nice to her, okay?"

"Noted." He nodded, feeling remorseful over the accident. If she was in a tight spot and desperate, it explained her response. The last thing he would ever do was truly harm a woman, even unintentionally.

"So, what do you have to report? Did you have a group of rowdy campers again?"

"No. My campers were great this time. In fact, I left them at reception so they could schedule a spring camping trip. I wanted to let you know that I spotted a lot of cougar and wolf tracks both near our camp site and on the trails. Plus, I think we're facing an epic snowstorm by Friday that the ranch needs to be prepared to batten down the hatches for."

Amber leaned back in her seat. "Damn. On both accounts. I will make sure Mav and Noah know to tell their people to keep an eye on the herds. Epic... how epic?"

"Enough that the cows should be moved into their winter lodgings between now and Friday morning. Otherwise, you'll end up losing far too many head, either to the storm or predators desperate for a meal in such extreme conditions. And you might want to have a man or two on guard at night. All the urban development is making the cougars, especially, more desperate."

"I know. Thanks for telling me. Now, if that's it, please go. No offense. But it's going to take all the air freshener I have to rid my office of the stench."

"That was it. But we might want to double check upcoming bookings. We should inform anyone scheduled to do a camping trip in the next two weeks that severe weather might disrupt their plans." He added the caveat because there was a lot he could handle, but he wouldn't needlessly put guests in harm's way. And thankfully, both Colt and now Amber agreed with him when he felt conditions were too severe to take guests out on camping trips. They were meant to be instructional and fun, and were dangerous enough with cougar, wolves, and bears roaming, they didn't need to add extreme weather to the mix. He and Sampson would survive just fine because he had been trained by the United States government to endure extreme weather conditions. The average person, though, wouldn't make it.

"I'll have reception check to see if there are any that are scheduled. With that in mind, for the time being, we can shift Eli and Matt to assist over at the stables instead of leading camping trips."

"Works for me. We're almost at the point in the year where we should stop doing the camping trips altogether, like we have in years prior. I can always give survival demos in the ballroom and help out in the stables too. But I'll tell those two to report to Mav tomorrow instead of me."

"Perfect. Oh, and Duncan, I've not said it before, but both Eli and Matt have been good additions to Silver Springs. Thanks for sending them my way."

"You're welcome, boss." He nodded at the compliment, whistled at Sampson, who rose from his spot on the floor, and headed out. Both Matt and Eli had served with Duncan under his command. They were good men, great soldiers, and had needed space—like he had after years of service.

On the first floor, he checked around for Eve. He spotted her near the front entrance. As he and Sampson passed, she glared like she would be only too happy to waterboard him for his crimes. His boots stuck and squeaked as he trod. He had no idea what she thought she was doing, but it certainly wasn't cleaning the damn floor.

He doubted she would last a week.

———

By the time Duncan and Sampson arrived at his place, fatigue was setting in but he pushed it away. There was far too much left for him to do this afternoon.

His cabin was one of the furthest away from the main hotel. After twelve years as a SEAL, he needed the wide-open spaces that living and working at Silver Springs Ranch afforded him. The cabin was completely off grid, with solar power and well water that was filtered.

There were two bedrooms, and a storage shed around back. He used the spare room to store all the gear he needed for leading camping trips. At least now, when he was outdoors, he had a tent and sleeping bag. He had spent far too many nights on the hard ground with only his backpack as a pillow.

He considered it a huge step up in the world. He was paid and paid well for the camping trips he led.

He kept Sampson outside while he carted all the gear into the spare bedroom. Tomorrow morning was soon enough to do an inventory of his supplies, and clean and repair any of the gear that needed it. Once he had everything in, he whistled for Sampson.

The dog came at a run from whatever it was he had been sniffing with avid interest in the yard. Could be anything, from wildlife droppings to the last place he'd taken a piss.

Sampson made a beeline for the couch.

"Halt. Just where do you think you're going?" He glared at the pup.

Sampson sent him a sheepish grin, like a kid that had been caught with his hand in the cookie jar.

"Nope. You're not sitting up there just yet. Come on." Duncan jerked his head toward the bedroom door.

Sampson whimpered.

"Well, if you would stop rolling in bear shit then you wouldn't need a bath. But you're not sitting on that couch smelling this bad."

Sampson lowered his head and slowly plodded toward the bedroom. Duncan rolled his eyes. "Come on, you rascal. It's not that bad. Once we're clean, we can make dinner."

Sampson's ears perked up at the mention of dinner.

One of the modifications Duncan had made to the cabin—with Colt's blessing—when he started at the ranch a few years back was to rip out the original bathtub and install a large, walk-in shower. There was a tub in the spare bathroom in the hall if he wanted a bath. But for his purposes, a big shower worked the best.

Duncan stripped in the bathroom, tossing his clothes in the hamper. Tomorrow would be soon enough to do a load of laundry. He held the glass door open for Sampson, who meekly trod into the enclosure.

He washed Sampson first, then let him out of the shower, where he lay on the rug while Duncan took his turn cleaning up. This way, Sampson would be somewhat dry by the time he was finished.

Between the two of them, it took a good hour for them both to get clean and dry. Duncan donned a pair of green sweats from his days in the Navy.

In the kitchen, he opened the fridge and almost groaned. Ms. Gregory, the hotel chef, was a fucking national treasure. There should be a monument built on ranch grounds to her. The woman treated him like he was one of her kids—kept an eye on his schedule, made sure he ate, and ensured his fridge was stocked with easy to heat up meals.

Boy, had she delivered. There was a large container of her bison chili, a full pan of lasagna, a bowl of salad with a note on it that he needed to eat his greens. And, lord love her, two big steaks, with heating instructions and potatoes au gratin.

"We're eating well tonight, pal." He pulled the steaks out, deciding to heat them in a pan over the stove as she suggested. He got the potatoes out as well.

While he was heating the potatoes and steaks up, he grabbed a beer and the salad too. He was hungry enough that anything would do. He prepared Sampson's bowl, and cut up half of one of the steaks to go on top of the kibble before he put the bowl on the ground.

"You've earned it, pal."

It wasn't until he was sitting at his kitchen table, plowing through the best meal he'd had in a week, that he thought about Eve. Well, to be honest, he had been thinking about finding some female company the following evening. He had a hankering for a good discipline session in Cabin X. It was a special cabin on the ranch, retrofitted with BDSM furniture, that he and his best friends used for their more illicit, dominant tastes.

But, hell, he had been busy enough with work here lately, what with training Matt and Eli, that it had been a month of Sundays since he had enjoyed the finer sex. After all his deployments, Duncan was all too familiar with long droughts of nothing but his hand for company —until he was on leave and could gorge himself on willing female flesh.

He could always head into town tomorrow night, see if Maribella was available after her shift. She was a good lay. And she didn't want any type of commitment from him—or any man that he knew about—which was the perfect type of hookup for him.

But when he thought about bedding a woman, for some lame reason, the new maid's furious image had popped into his brain. She definitely had some fire in her. It was too damn bad she was an employee, because he wouldn't dawdle with someone who worked on the ranch. No dipping his wick in the company ink for him, no matter how sweet her ass was.

Still, he'd be lying if he said he hadn't considered what she looked like naked. Not that he was interested in finding out that little kernel. He wouldn't ask or do anything where she was concerned.

No, that little maid had trouble written all over her cute behind. It would be much better if he found a tourist passing through to satiate his needs, even if it was only in the vanilla sense of things.

Because he would bet Eve was a lot like her name-sake—that one in the garden tempting Adam to bite the apple and, if he touched her, he would be expelled from his own personal Eden.

3

*B*y the end of her first week, Eve felt like she had gotten the hang of her duties—for the most part. That didn't include the day she had over-loaded one of the washing machines, or the time she forgot to stock the third-floor rooms with toilet paper.

She had moved past those instances. Those mistakes were learning experiences. Ones she wouldn't repeat.

But if she finished her duties quickly enough today, they were letting the majority of the staff leave early on account of the blizzard heading their way.

A damn blizzard!

She had never been in a snowstorm of that magnitude. Hell, in Georgia, on the rare occasions that they would get a light dusting of snow, the entire city and state would shut down.

But here they were forecasting feet of snow—as in multiple. Thankfully, Eve had gone to the grocery store two days ago, when the forecast models began warning of the impending storm. She'd spent the remainder of the cash she had until her first paycheck next week, and stocked up, figuring she would head home and whip up a batch of white chicken chili to help her weather the storm.

It was also why she was moving from room to room as fast as possible before the storm made its presence felt. Granted, her cabin wasn't that far away from the main hotel, but the thought of navigating the small mountain roads covered in snow gave her the willies. In each room she visited, she focused on the task at hand, running through a mental checklist and marking off each task as complete. She had to, otherwise she would forget to add extra toiletries or restock the mini fridge.

For the most part, she didn't mind the work. It kept her busy. While physically taxing, it gave her time to think and plan, because the ranch was rapidly becoming a place where she really believed she could make a go of it. She doubted Trevor had caught her trail after all the zigzagging she had done.

And it gave her hope when she had been without it for so long, she almost didn't recognize the emotion.

She entered room 304 after knocking, announcing, "Room Service," and receiving no response from inside. Most of the guests had left early, either yesterday or first thing this morning, when news of the storm broke. Granted, there were a few stalwarts who planned to ride the blizzard out.

Eve thought those people were crazy. But, to each his or her own.

After stripping the bedding and collecting all the trash, she gathered up the toiletries she'd noted that needed to be restocked on her initial foray into the room.

A strong hand grabbed her shoulder from behind. She yelped in shock. Startled, she tossed everything she held in her hands up into the air before it rained down on the carpeted floor at her feet. Fear infused every molecule of her existence. Her heart pounded wildly in her chest. Gasping at the runaway panic flooding her system, she swiveled around with her fists raised, ready to fight, to defend herself. Trevor couldn't be here, could he?

But it wasn't her nightmare. *Thank God!*

It was the man who was slowly but surely on a path to become the bane of her existence. His name was Duncan. She knew this not because he had told her that, but because she had asked Jessica at reception after their initial run in.

"Relax. I didn't mean to scare you," he murmured calmly, assessing her in that way of his that seemed to pierce through all the body armor she wore around herself like a cloak to uncover what lay beneath.

His eyes were so dark a brown, they seemed black. He had a strong nose that was slightly crooked, as if it had been broken a time or two, and full, kissable lips that were turned down at the corners as he studied her reaction—as if he was dissecting every minute detail and filing it away for later. His firm jaw was covered with a few days' growth of dark stubble, and shrouded lips that she had thought about far too much these past few days. Dark chocolate tufts of hair stuck out from beneath his ballcap and curled at the ends. For some insane reason, she itched to touch those curls, and find out if they were as soft as they looked, especially on a man who radiated confident strength.

With a hand over her chest to calm the rapid beating of her heart, she blasted him. "Do you do this often? Sneak up on people and scare the daylights out of them?"

For the first time in forever, she hadn't been paying attention to her surroundings. She had dropped her guard. Begun to get comfortable with the routine she had established the last few days. But really, how stupid could she be? Trevor was still out there, gunning for her, searching for the opportunity to find her and end her sorry existence.

Duncan shrugged, and the muscles beneath his gray flannel rippled, broadcasting his powerful build. "Habit. Retired military. I spent twelve years of my life being trained and ordered to be stealthy."

Retired military? That explained his confident bearing, the way he stood as if ready for action at a moment's notice. With a furious glare, she knelt and started collecting all the items she'd dropped in her fright, all while trying to ignore the testosterone pouring off him and what it did to her on a very feminine level. A sensation curled in her belly that she'd not experienced in so long, she almost didn't recognize it had surfaced inside her—desire. It made her wonder what it would feel like to touch that strength.

Duncan crouched down on his heels beside her, reminding her just how big he was, dwarfing her with his size. He was crowding her to the point that she could feel the warmth of his body heat, and notice that subtle masculine scent of his that, unlike in their first meeting, left her wanting to get closer and inhale him. His near-ness caused the tension in her system to ratchet up a few notches, turning her insides into liquid, pulsing need. He reached for the supplies on the floor, like he was trying to help.

But before he could pick up the toilet paper roll, she snatched it up, absolutely furious with herself for allowing his presence to rile her. Through clenched teeth, she muttered, "I've got it."

She hated that he made her feel territorial with her space. But his nearness was twisting her up inside—after scaring her. All her wires were getting crossed because there was no way she could be attracted to the big guy.

"Let me help. It was my mistake," he replied, calm as a still lake, and sincere in his contrition. There was no malice or mocking in his gaze. Just a steady strength and serenity.

"I said, I've got it. Is there something you need?" She didn't want to warm up to him—or anyone, really, at the ranch. It would be far too dangerous to her wellbeing to let down her guard that way. The only way she would remain hidden and safe was to keep people at a distance.

And she sure as hell didn't trust her judgement enough where men were concerned. Why would she? She had allowed a man close once. Someone she thought she could trust—love, even—and it had destroyed her entire life.

What was more, she needed Duncan to go away before the shaking and panic overwhelmed her. It was an atavistic response in her circuitry. The aftermath of the fear as it retreated from her system. Because she couldn't let anyone see how weak she had become. How much something so simple affected her.

"I wanted to apologize again for the other day."

She nodded, avoiding eye contact, and attempting to breathe deeply to waylay the gurgling mess of her belly. "Fine. Thanks. You can go now."

She tried to swallow it down, really, she did. It happened every time she had an incident that frightened her. It brought back the night that changed everything: the fear of being strangled, the blood that had been on her hands after fighting Trevor off. It left her sweating and quaking while she battled the nausea. The room began to spin in a seesaw fashion.

And for some unknown reason, Duncan wasn't leaving, increasing Eve's surging panic until it dominated every part of her being, even quashing the flash of desire.

Why the hell was he still crouched at her side? Why wasn't he leaving her alone, dammit?

Did he know who she really was? Had they crossed paths before? She sucked in a shaky breath at the terrifying thought.

No. She would have remembered meeting someone like him even if the encounter had been momentary as she served him breakfast, because his dominating presence saturated the space. At the mere thought of food, bile clamored up her esophagus and overpowered her feeble attempts toward control.

Fear won.

On a groan, she doubled over and puked her guts out, dry heaving until there was nothing left in her stomach. Tears streamed down her face as her stomach clenched and revolted. Some splashed over Duncan's boots, given his proximity.

"Jesus Christ! What the hell? Are you all right? If you're ill, you should be home in bed," he scolded, finally shifting away.

It was his fault to begin with. If he hadn't frightened her, and had just left her be, it never would have happened.

Wiping her mouth with the back of her hand, she muttered, "I'm sorry. When I'm frightened, it happens sometimes. Stay where you are."

Eve rose on shaky, trembling legs. She hated giving in to the nausea. It always left her hollowed out. Grimacing, she grabbed a towel from her cart then knelt at his rather large feet and wiped his boots clean. They were military style black boots, and didn't seem worse for wear. She wiped up every spot on the black she found. Thank goodness there had been little but water in her belly.

When she'd finished cleaning off Duncan's boots, she glanced up, taking in his powerfully built thighs and flat belly. The man didn't have an ounce of fat on him, likely due to his stint in the military. "Truly, I am sorry."

He held a hand out for her to take. He had long, thick fingers, and a wide palm. Without thinking, she placed her hand in his and sucked in a sharp breath when those powerful fingers closed around it. It felt like she was touching a downed electrical wire with the energy radiating through the simple contact as he helped her to her feet.

He cast her a lopsided grin. "Let's call it a draw and

say we're even. Truly, I didn't mean to scare you. Are you certain that you're not sick?"

"I'm fine." Other than she'd have to scrub the carpet after he left—and was beyond mortified with embarrassment. Not to mention, she had most likely completely lost her mind, considering she couldn't help but wonder what those strong hands would feel like on other parts of her body.

But other than that, she was just peachy.

He exuded warmth and vigor. Kind concern filled his dark gaze. "If you're sure, I will leave you to your work."

He made her want to lean in and absorb some of his strength. It made him dangerous. Putting space between them, she nodded. "I am."

"Don't linger too long. It's already beginning to snow."

Damn.

For a moment, she had forgotten all about the snowstorm. Forgotten about everything really, except for him. But that was part of being around Duncan, he eclipsed everything else. "I only have a few rooms left before heading home."

He studied her for another minute, like he wasn't convinced she was fine, until he finally conceded with a slight nod. "Be safe."

"You too," Eve murmured.

Duncan left without a backward glance. She watched him stride away. Those powerful legs put distance between them with ease. He moved with a sinuous grace for such a large man. Gazing after him, she marveled at his broad back and the way his jeans cupped a behind molded to make women everywhere swoon.

Eve didn't relax until he boarded the elevator, leaving her alone on the third floor. She didn't like the way he affected her. He stirred her in elemental ways that she hadn't felt in years. Made her hunger for his touch even when she wanted to smack him for crowding her and scaring her.

Attempting to put the incident and sinful man out of her mind, she focused her energy on the remaining work she needed to accomplish, hurrying through her tasks. It worked, for the most part, mainly because she didn't want to get stranded in the approaching storm.

———

Eve was something all right.

Duncan had never witnessed such abject terror on a woman's face before. Well, not since the horrific, bloody streets of Kabul, but that had been war. Nor was he comfortable with the way she made him want to chase away those dark terrors, protect her from whatever demons pursued her, whether real or imagined.

Amber had been correct in her assumption about Eve the other day.

The woman seemed lost and alone, a wounded bird in dire need of rescuing. No one was more surprised than Duncan by the punch of lust he'd experienced with her kneeling at his feet.

It showed how much of a sick fuck he had become. The woman had puked all over his feet moments before and yet, when she had stared up at him with those big golden eyes rimmed with moisture, he'd pictured those sinful lips surrounding his dick and watching as she sucked him off.

He was a sick fucking bastard. There was little doubt of that, not after everything he had witnessed, experienced, and done while serving in the Navy.

But those eyes of hers killed him. The fear, the resolve, and the display of spine when she remembered she had one, all combined to make her a fascinating mixture of fragility and fierceness. The combination was a knockout punch to his equilibrium.

It made Duncan want to extend his protection. Made him want to possess her and discover if the flashes of fire he spied would ignite in the bedroom.

And that made her as dangerous as a grenade with the pin removed.

Duncan didn't do relationships. He had sex. He loved indulging in women's soft flesh with the smooth textures and tastes, the feel of their lush forms beneath him or bound to a St. Andrew's Cross. Every now and then he thoroughly enjoyed a torrid, sex-infused night with a tourist, or one of a bevy of locals at the Bucking Bronco. Some he even took to Cabin X to indulge in his darker desires.

There was little he liked more than tying up a willing woman and fucking her blind.

That Eve had crossed his mind—what she would look like bound for his pleasure, with desire filling her gold gaze—made him realize just how dangerous she could be. His best course of action was cutting as wide a berth around the confounded woman as humanly possible. The less interaction he had with her, the better off he would be.

Relationships were akin to prison shackles. He'd watched it destroy his parents with his dad's staunchly erected apathy, and his mom's broken-hearted descent into an extra-marital affair that had destroyed the tenuous foundation of their family.

Duncan spent the next few hours helping the hotel staff prepare for the extreme weather as the bulk of the storm barreled in like a son of a bitch. Before he headed home, he double checked that Eve had already left the hotel for the day.

Christ, it wasn't his job to look after her. Not when he'd vowed to stay away from her. He could only shake his head at himself for his inability to remove her presence from his thoughts as he drove home in near white out conditions.

Once the storm had moved on and finished dumping its fury over the ranch, he and the rest of the guys would spend a day or two with plows and shovels, clearing the roads and walkways, making the ranch byways safe for residents and tourists alike. But until then, he and Sampson were home bound.

And in the meantime, he would stop thinking about Eve and the sinful, seductive image of her kneeling at his feet.

4

———

The blizzard was unlike anything Eve had ever seen. The sheer volume of snow that had fallen over the past forty-eight hours was mindboggling. By the time she made it to her cabin on Friday afternoon, there were already two inches of snow coating the ground.

And she wasn't even going to think about the short drive in her beat-up truck with balding tires from the hotel to the cabin.

Next time, she was walking. It would be far cheaper for her to invest in snow gear than in new tires. Granted, she would add new tires to her growing list of things to purchase over the next few months, should working at the hotel pan out in the long term.

Since she had walked through the door on Friday afternoon, ready to kiss the ground after her tense drive, another thirty-five inches had fallen.

Thirty-five inches over two days.

It was insane. It had snowed without stopping until this morning.

Now that the storm had passed, the sun peeked out from behind lingering cloud cover. The world outside her front door had this quiet stillness to it with the pristine snow.

It was beautiful. Achingly so.

But the storm brought with it subzero temperatures. Eve had never been this cold in her life. The heater was pumping out as much warmth as possible. If she could figure out how to get the flue open in the fireplace, she'd get a fire going. But sadly, she hadn't figured that one out yet.

Since she had been homebound the last two days, she had baked cinnamon muffins, lemon bars, jalapeño cheddar cornbread, and chocolate chip cookies. As soon as she could afford it, she planned on investing in an e-reader, otherwise she would need to buy bigger clothes if all she did in her spare time was bake.

And while she had spent the better part of yesterday baking, she had also made a big stock pot full of white chicken chili. It paired well with the spicy cornbread—so much so that it should be criminal.

She had gotten a message from the hotel an hour ago that they were planning a late start on Monday for all workers until the roads were cleared and safer for travel, which she thoroughly appreciated. It meant she got to sleep until eight instead of rising at six when it was still pitch black out.

Still, she was left wondering how the hell she was going to clean her truck off. The damn thing was buried beneath feet of snow. Rather idiotically on her part, when she'd taken the job, she had never considered the supplies she would need for freezing temperatures and blizzards. Which proved how desperate she had become. She'd found the job listing while eating breakfast in Denver and contemplating her next move. When she'd figured out the remoteness of the ranch, she'd imagined it was the perfect place to hide, and gone for it, never once considering all that would come with it.

But she would learn. She would prepare. And she'd ensure she was never caught unawares ever again.

Added to her ever-expanding list of items to purchase were a yoga mat and some weights. That way, she wouldn't be sitting around all winter in her cabin, eating baked goods, as pleasant and indulgent as that might sound. While she did have a job that was rather physical, if in her free time all she did was sit and eat, they would have to roll her out of the cabin come spring. Resuming some manner of physical fitness routine would be good for her.

But those things weren't what brought her over to the window. She peered through the curtains, trying to remain hidden.

Someone was out there. Out in the small drive of her cabin, moving around. A person would have to be crazy or a criminal to be outside in weather like this—or very possibly, both.

It was hard to believe that out here in the boonies she had to worry about being robbed or having her vehicle stolen—or worse. Eve knew all too well the monster in the closet could be so much worse. And the thought that her little hideaway might no longer be safe left her spiraling.

Had Trevor found her at the hotel? Seen her there and finally tracked her down, delayed only because of the storm?

She hated the debilitating fear slithering through her belly. Loathed the way her hands shook. Detested that what she wanted to do most was hide out in the bathroom until whoever it was had left.

But then, if it was Trevor, he wouldn't leave until she was dead. With her car buried beneath feet of snow and no neighbor close by, she had to rely on herself for her survival. Putting her sneakers on, she mentally added a pair of snow boots to her list of things to buy, then grabbed her coat and hat. But before she headed outside to confront the lout disturbing her hard-fought peace, she grabbed her cell phone and shoved it in her coat pocket, then made a short trip to the nightstand.

Removing the gun, she double checked the subcompact Beretta, ensuring the clip was properly loaded in the nine-millimeter. If Trevor wanted to kill her, she wasn't going down without a fight.

She could still hear whoever was outside. They certainly weren't being quiet in their approach. Trying to be as stealthy as possible, she opened the front door inch by inch, sucking in a deep breath at the arctic blast of cold air. Creeping outside, she plodded through the pile of snow as if she was walking on eggshells.

She reached the driveway, and fought the urge to puke. She was surprised her heart hadn't beat its way clear out of her chest in her fright. With the gun in one hand, she laid a steadying hand on the truck.

Whoever was here, they were on the other side of her truck. She wiped the window but the snow made it impossible to see who was there. All she got was the impression of a large male figure.

Swallowing the terror dogging her footsteps, Eve rounded the truck's hood until the man came into view. She couldn't tell what he had in his hands, only that it was long. Holding the handgun steady, she lifted it, removed the safety, and pointed it at the broad back not ten feet away.

"Who the hell are you? And what are you doing here?" She was proud that her voice didn't waver or show any signs of the dread infusing her being as the intruder's identity remained unknown.

The man turned slowly, like he wasn't in a hurry to answer the question. When she recognized the scowling alpha with the dark brown gaze, she almost sagged with relief. Trevor hadn't found her yet. *Thank God!*

"Honey, put the gun down. I'm just clearing the snow from your driveway, and was going to clean off your truck for you too." Duncan stood with his hands up in a calm fashion. But his gaze beneath the bill of his ballcap was sharp, and trained on the Beretta.

Putting the safety back on, she lowered the firearm. "Sorry. I didn't know who was out here."

Duncan cocked his head and asked, "Do you always approach people with a loaded gun?"

She sputtered, feeling foolish, "No. I've never even

shot the gun before, I just... thought it might be someone else."

"Who?" That assessing gaze of his was back and narrowed on her, like he was attempting to divine all her secrets.

"A thief, or burglar, or I don't know, someone who escaped from prison, bent on mischief."

"Honey, you would know because they would have been at your front door, not wielding a snow plow."

That was what was in his hands! Mortified, she wished a hole would open up for her to crawl in and pretend like the last few minutes hadn't happened. "Point taken."

"Well, if that's all you need, I'm going to get back to this, as I have a few more cabins to dig out before I can head home for the day."

She nodded and started to turn but then blurted, "When you're done, if you'd like, I was about to have some lunch. I've got some chili that might warm you up a bit before you head off to your next stop."

Duncan regarded her for a moment. "That's mighty nice of you. I don't have too long, but a warm meal would be much appreciated."

She cast him a tremulous smile. Feeding him was the least she could do after letting her fear get the better of her. What must he think of her? Between throwing up on his boots and pointing a loaded gun at him, she had never had this many blunders around a single individual in her life. Not even when she had been waiting tables with handsy men trying to cop a feel while her hands were weighed down with a full tray.

Contrite, embarrassed, she trudged through the snow back to the front door of the cabin. If she was going to have company for lunch, she was going to do it up right. After stowing the gun back in the nightstand drawer, Eve set the table and decided to brew a pot of coffee. If she had been outside working in this weather, she would desire as many hot things as possible to warm herself up, and she doubted Duncan liked hot tea.

Once the small dinette table was set, she got the coffee brewing. The pungent aroma of the coffee filled the kitchen. Then she decided to heat the chili over the stove instead of in the microwave. She ladled enough for two bowls into the pot but then decided to add a bit more. He was such a big man. She doubted a single bowl would be enough to fill him up.

She got the chili simmering over the stove and, as it heated, she cut a few pieces of cornbread and arranged them on a plate. Because she was feeling super guilty about the gun incident, she put some cookies on another small plate as well. Men liked cookies and baked goods, right?

At the knock on the door, she startled.

She was an idiot, acting like she didn't know he was coming to the door. Straightening her spine, she marched to the door and opened it with a smile.

Duncan was infinitely the most alpha man of her acquaintance. It wasn't just his body and face, but his presence. Most likely his time in the military had instilled that quality in him.

He perused her form in her oversized sweater and form-fitting jeans without the coat shielding her body.

She shivered, and told herself it was from the cold and not the man. She didn't have time for distractions with men, no matter how much his presence affected her. "Come in."

"Not going to shoot me for trespassing, are you?"

Embarrassment flooded her. But then she realized he was joking. The tension fled. She chuckled halfheartedly. "No. Not today, at least."

"Good enough." He entered, instantly suffusing the cabin with his potent masculine energy.

While she shut the door, he removed his coat and hung it beside hers and then removed his boots as well without her asking.

"Everything is ready if you want to have a seat at the table. I made a fresh pot of coffee too."

"It smells great. Coffee sounds like heaven."

She hurried past him into the kitchen and poured him a cup. "How do you take it? I have cream and sugar."

"Black is fine." He followed her into the kitchen, even more silent on his feet in just socks.

Screwing up her courage, she turned and handed him the coffee mug. "Ah, why don't you have a seat? I'll bring the pot over to the table so you can help yourself."

She was desperately trying not to fidget under his frank stare. He took a long sip of his coffee, all while gazing at her. It made her self-conscious. Did she have some dirt on her face? Was her hair a tangled mess?

When he'd finished drinking, he nodded and strode over to the dinette table.

She already had a stone trivet in position on the table. Wiping her hands on her jeans, she carried the pot and serving spoon over to the table. She served him first and then added some to her own bowl before setting the pot with the remainder on the trivet.

"It smells amazing. You made this?"

"Yeah. I like to cook. Although, I'm more of a baker than a cook. But I love a good chili during the winter months."

She waited with bated breath as he tried a bite. Surprised pleasure splashed across his face. "Damn, it's really good."

Relief flooded her as he lit into the meal with gusto. She ate sparingly. She was hungry, but her nerves were dominating her hunger at the moment. It had been over a year since she had shared a meal with someone. Funny how she hadn't realized how much she had missed having interaction with other people. She had been too concerned with survival to even think about it.

"So, you mentioned that you were in the military."

Duncan regarded her across the small table. "Yep. Navy."

"And what did you do in the Navy?"

"SEAL Lieutenant with my own platoon."

Whoa! That explained him. He hadn't just been military but an elite military officer. "How does a former Navy SEAL wind up in the middle of Colorado doing, well... I don't really know what it is you do for the ranch."

He smiled then, an unguarded, full smile that transformed his face. She felt her panties go damp. "During my last year of service, I was on leave for a few weeks. Rode my Harley through the mountains and stopped in Winter Park for a couple days. A few of the guys from the ranch were getting into a scuffle at this local watering hole, and I helped them out. There was this pack of tourists who couldn't hold their liquor and had become downright offensive toward all the bar staff and patrons. When the guys stepped in to defend one of the waitresses, I helped. Afterward, I got to talking with Colt. He's Amber's brother, and used to run the joint. He offered me a job if I wanted it, when I was done with my service."

"And what is it that you do?"

"I oversee camping trips and teach outdoor survival training for most of the year, until it's too cold for normal people to camp. When it's required, I also volunteer with the local Mountain Search and Rescue Team. We tend to get tourists who don't know jack about surviving in the wild who get lost or injured from time to time."

"Ah, so you can take the guy out of the military but not the military out of the guy."

"Something like that." He smiled, wiping his mouth, and set the napkin on the table. "Thank you for the meal. Is there a reason you don't have a fire going in the fireplace? It would help heat the cabin up for you considerably."

She winced at the question, and her own incompetence. "I couldn't figure out how to get the flue open. I think it's jammed or something."

"Let me take a look before I head out." He rose and headed over to the fireplace. He moved the screen aside and bent down. She watched him, and found herself admiring his backside.

"I see what the problem is, the flue lever is a bit

jammed. Might need to be replaced. It's open now, so you shouldn't have any problem building a fire. I'll tell Lincoln to come take a look at it sometime this week. He's the head of maintenance, and can get it fixed for you."

"Thank you so much. I've been freezing. If you would like to take the cookies with you, in case you get hungry while you're working, I can put them in a to go bag for you." It was strange, because once she had gotten him talking, her nerves had settled, and she felt comfortable with him. Safe, even.

"Sure, I'll take a few. I won't turn cookies down, especially if they're as good as your chili."

"They're better," she blurted, and then blushed. She headed into the kitchen, grabbed a small brown paper bag, and put all the cookies that were on the plate inside.

"I don't need that many."

"I want you to have them. Otherwise, I will eat them all and you'll be using the plow to lift me out of here."

He laughed, making crinkle lines appear at the corners of his eyes, and she could only think: damn. He was hot as hell, and a total badass to boot. It was a wicked combination that had her twisted up inside. "Fair enough."

"I should get you some of the muffins too."

"The cookies are enough. Besides, I really need to get back out there pronto if I'm going to get all the cabins on my list finished today."

"Okay." She trailed him over to the door, rather disappointed that he was leaving. She felt safe enough with him around that there was a part of her that didn't want him to go. Was she really that starved for company and human contact?

She stared at his jean-clad ass as he bent down and shoved his boots back on. Good God, the man had a mighty fine backside. A girl could bounce a quarter off his bum. It wasn't flat either, like so many men had, but firmly rounded.

"Thanks again for lunch." He shrugged into his coat and nimbly buttoned the front.

She handed him the cookies. His fingers brushed hers as he took the bag. She felt his touch down to the soles of her feet. It was like a lightning strike. Violent. Illuminating. And left her vibrating with the aftershocks. "Stay warm."

He nodded. "Do me a favor. Promise me that you won't go waving that gun around until you've been properly trained to use it."

She couldn't promise him that. Because when Trevor came for her, which he would eventually, she would have no other choice but to use it. Yet, he was right. She needed to get trained on the firearm. There just hadn't been time since she'd bought it. She'd been too busy running and hiding to learn. But that would change now.

So she lied, and hated herself for doing so. "I promise. Cross my heart."

"Be careful if you decide to head out today. The roads are absolute shit, and slick as can be."

"I'm not leaving until work tomorrow."

"Good enough." He nodded and headed out.

Eve watched him walk away and climb into his truck. She closed the front door after he'd backed out of the drive, still in shock. She'd felt a sexual tug of awareness, of need and desire for a man.

Was it because she was finally in a place where she might be able to explore the possibility, or was it him? She wasn't sure. She would need more time to discern the truth. Which was ironic given that she was laden with nothing but lies.

5

*B*y Friday, most of the snow had melted and temperatures had crept back up into the forties by day, and thirties overnight. Cold, but Duncan had been in worse spots, and colder on missions.

His former SEAL buddies Matt and Eli sat with him in the hotel meeting room. Matt had left the corps a year ago, burned out and battling some fairly hefty PTSD. Duncan had made the guy an offer of employment six months ago, figuring this was a place where he could begin to heal. There were parts of their time spent in the Navy that would live with them forever. Far too many instances had happened to be able to bury them completely.

And when you returned to civilian life, adjusting, feeling like you were part of society at large once again, was on par with landing on an alien planet.

It was jarring. You didn't fit in, not like you did with the members of your platoon. And it was difficult, especially at first, to connect with others. Unless you've been in it, experienced the horrors of war for years on end, there's no way to truly empathize.

"Matt, you got the Miller party on Monday for a five-day stretch. Make sure to take the SAT phone in case of bad weather. There's a possibility of some more snow late next week that we will need to keep an eye on," Duncan stated, glancing at his buddy.

"We should be fine, even if it's cold as shit," Matt commented with a shrug. He'd grown his dirty blond hair out since leaving the Navy. It was almost at his shoulders now. He claimed women loved it.

Eli snorted. "Not as cold as our stints in Alaskan waters. You're just growing soft in your old age."

Duncan shot Eli a look, assessing the former sniper. He'd kept his military short buzz cut. "Eli, there are two single overnights I want you to man, since I'm also going to be on a trip for four days. Think you can handle them?"

"I've got you covered. By now, we both know the drill. Like you told us last May, easy money compared to what we were used to." Eli shrugged. He'd gotten out about six months after Duncan but had taken a dark turn for a while there. He'd found himself at the bottom of a bottle for a good eighteen months before losing everything and deciding to sober up.

Since he had been at the ranch, Duncan's buddy had become an invaluable asset, never eschewing the grunt work, and seemed to relish his new lease on life.

"Good. We're in that time of year when the camping trips begin to dwindle. January and February especially are long, cold, snowy months. We'll be working mainly with Maverick and Noah, filling in and helping them out at the stables and barn."

"Shoveling shit, no doubt. But at least it will put us closer to those meals Ms. Gregory makes for the staff," Eli said.

"Not to mention the available women passing through. Have you guys seen the newest recruit, Eve?" Matt said, and wiggled his brows.

"I did the other day. Tiny thing. Woman has a fine pair of legs on her," Eli commented with a nod.

Duncan didn't comment, he just listened as they listed her attributes. He couldn't deny that Eve was a looker.

"She's pretty damn hot. Wouldn't mind having her ride me reverse cowgirl. So I can watch her stellar ass bounce on my balls," Matt said with a chuckle, and a glimmer in his eyes.

"Yeah, she looks like she could give a guy quite the ride. I've considered making a play for her. See if she would be up for a good time," Eli commented rather thoughtfully, as if he had given the idea more than a passing consideration.

"I have, as well. What about you, Duncan? Going to make a play for the maid?" Matt asked with a raised brow.

"Woman's a menace," Duncan muttered, recalling the way she had pointed a gun at him last Sunday. Women were normally much more accommodating where he was concerned. And ever since that interaction, he had made it a point to steer clear of Eve. She was too much of an interesting mix of strength and fragility. It made him wonder about her past. There was something she was running from. It was more drama than he wanted in his life. He liked peace and comfort.

Ever since their initial meeting, the woman had decimated his peace of mind. Furthering any type of relationship with her—whether benign or not—would be a horrible move on his part.

Matt snorted and shook his head. "So that's a no for our indomitable leader. That leaves it between you and me, Eli."

Eli smirked. "I'll flip you for it."

"Please, that's too easy. Game of five card stud, winner gets to make a move," Matt offered, as if they were deciding what movie they should watch, or whether to head to Park Tavern or the Bucking Bronco, and not who got to make a pass at Eve.

"She's not a goddamn piece of meat to be divvied up between you two blockheads. Best keep in mind that you're not the only men on the ranch, either, there are Tanner and Lincoln, not to mention the rest of the wranglers, and a town full of men. Woman has her pick," Duncan snapped, not sure why he cared. The woman could date and sleep with whomever she wanted. It was no skin off his nose.

"Are you sweet on her or something? I've never known you to defend a woman's honor before," Eli said with avid interest.

Duncan grunted as a response. His relationship—or lack of one—with Eve was no one's business but his.

"I still think it should be a toss-up between the two of us, Eli. Duncan's opted out for whatever reason. Never known him to take on a vow of chastity or abstinence, but whatever. I'm game for a poker match to see who gets to try and woo her first," Matt stated.

Eli shook Matt's hand. "You're on. And if she shoots down whoever wins the hand, the loser gets to try for her."

"Deal," Matt replied.

"Oh for fuck's sake, sailors, we're here to discuss work, not your dicks and whichever hole you want to stick it in. If you guys fuck up, it's not just your asses on the line, but mine too. Either get your shit together, or get out. If you want to duke it out over Eve, be my guests—when you're not on the clock," Duncan snarled, itching to knock their heads together to instill some sense into them.

"Sorry. We'll behave," Matt countered.

"Yeah, didn't mean to piss you off. You feeling all right there, Duncan?"

"Fine. Just want to get this shit taken care of so I can head home." He had plans to go into town tonight and find Maribella for a scene. He needed to get his dick thinking about someone other than Eve. The busty blonde waitress at Park Tavern was just the ticket.

"We're good on our assignments for next week. Right, Eli?"

"That we are." Eli rolled his eyes, his exasperation with Duncan clear.

That only added fuel to the fire of his anger. Duncan nodded and shoved his chair back. "Good. And please don't make a big deal out of the competition the two of you have for the maid. I don't need Amber breathing down my neck because you two stepped out of line with an employee."

"Sir, yes, sir." Matt saluted.

Eli stood and mimicked Matt's salute. The fucker.

"I'm heading out. See that you keep it in your pants." Duncan strode out of the meeting room, with Matt and Eli chuckling behind him.

He didn't know why it burned him that they were going to make a play for Eve. He wanted to tell them they weren't her type. But who was he to say what kind of guy she liked to date? It wasn't his job or responsibility to keep the wolves from sniffing around her skirts.

So why the fuck did he feel so territorial?

She wasn't his submissive. The woman didn't belong to him in any way.

And yet, beneath the surface was this caveman mentality of wanting to drag her out of the hotel and take her to his cabin to ensure no other man touched her. But that was a level of commitment that made him want to continue to cut a wide berth around her. It meant no more accepting her invitation for lunch, no more checking to make sure her truck had been cleared of snow.

With his day over now that he had finished up the meeting with Matt and Eli, he headed straight for his truck. Time to get his game face on and get serious about heading into town tonight.

A night with Maribella should rid him of his obsession with Eve. Get her out of his system so that he wasn't lying in bed at night imagining what she looked like naked and bound for his pleasure. This way, he would stop wondering if she was a screamer when she came, or if her cries of ecstasy were sweetly uttered gasps.

It was why he was going to ask Maribella to come to Cabin X with him. That way, he could slake his darker lusts on her busty form.

Cabin X looked like all the other cabins on the property, but Duncan and his buddies had modified it on the inside, turning it into a sex dungeon with a plethora of BDSM furniture. His cabin was the closest to Cabin X. He passed by it every day on his way to and from work—when he wasn't leading a camping excursion, anyway.

As he started to pass by it on the small two lane back road, he spied a familiar face, and slammed on the brakes.

"Son of a bitch! What the hell is the woman doing?"

Backing his truck up, he turned into the drive just as she entered the cabin like she owned the place. He reaffirmed his earlier comment. The woman was a menace, and clearly needed a lesson in manners. He should tan her hide for trespassing where she didn't belong.

When he'd parked out front and climbed out, he said to Sampson in the truck bed, "Stay here, bud, I'll be right back out."

Scowling, he marched toward the door. Eve was about to get a lesson she wouldn't soon forget. But Sampson chose that moment not to listen to his orders, and raced past him inside the cabin the moment he pushed the door open.

Fuck. Apparently, this was going to be a group effort.

$\mathcal{O}$n her day off, it was warm enough to head outside. Eve decided to get a better lay of the land for a couple of reasons. One, she would be better prepared to escape his clutches, should Trevor find her, if she knew where to go on the ranch. Two, she figured the exercise couldn't hurt, and would help her body acclimate better to the altitude. And three, she was tired of looking at the four walls of her cabin on her days off, with nothing to do but bake. This way, she would get some exercise instead of baking up a batch of scones and stuffing her face all night.

The air was crisp and cool. She bundled up as best she could, figuring she would head to Winter Park tomorrow morning and find a better winter coat that was more suited to the mountains than the threadbare tan peacoat she had on. It was a cold day for a hike, but it would clear out the cobwebs in her brain.

Two weeks on the ranch thus far, and not a single sighting of Trevor. It meant she was starting to relax, starting to believe that this could be her place, her new home.

Being from the south, she wasn't the biggest fan of the cold or the snow like they'd had last weekend. However, if being here meant she could stop looking over her shoulder every five minutes then she would brave the cold and snow.

She made mental notes of different landmarks along the road. She didn't want to get lost and be unable to find her way home.

Funny thing, that, her cabin was beginning to feel like home. She had begun to have ideas for decorating the cabin, like buying some extra pillows and bed sheets, an extra thick blanket or two for the nights that were frigid and left her shivering under the covers.

After she had been walking for a while, she started to feel the need to pee. So much so that her bladder began protesting. Dammit, she would never make it home in time, either.

She rounded a curve and spied a cabin a little ways off the road a bit.

Oh, thank goodness!

Surely the guest or employee would let her use their bathroom. Not that she couldn't find a bush in the woods, but it was cold, and there was still snow in some patches. The last thing she wanted to do was drop her pants so all and sundry could see her ass, not that there was anyone out here. But with the way her luck tended to go, she would drop trow and that would be the time that a huge group of hikers passed by.

Spying relief in sight, she quickened her pace to the

cabin. The exterior looked like a carbon copy of hers, if a bit larger. At the front door, she knocked loudly. Then waited. And waited some more.

She knocked again, this time more forcefully. "Hello," she shouted. "I hate to bother you, but I really need a bathroom."

Eve shifted from foot to foot as her bladder reached near bursting levels.

When she'd knocked a second time without anyone answering, she wondered if perhaps this was a guest cabin, and empty. Even better. She tried the handle.

Luck appeared to be on her side today because the door opened.

Eve didn't hesitate. She rushed inside, barely sparing a glance around, and made a beeline for the bathroom.

After she'd relieved herself, she noticed that the bathroom had handcuffs attached to the toilet. There were silver metal rings sticking out from the wall.

What the hell kind of bathroom was this?

She walked back into the living area. There was furniture—big wooden and leather pieces, but it was unlike any furniture she had ever seen before. Curious, she examined one of the pieces, running her hands over the leather bench with all its various silver loops. She fingered one of them, not understanding what exactly she was looking at.

The most normal piece of furniture was the wooden armoire. Trying to puzzle out exactly what this place was, she opened doors and drawers. Inside, there was a motherload of condoms, lubricant, leather whips, butt plugs, bullet vibrators... and it finally dawned on her.

This was a sex dungeon.

She turned, and looked at the furniture with new eyes. She couldn't help but imagine what it would feel like to be restrained while having a man do all sorts of erotic things with her body. Her belly tightened, and an image of Duncan looking badass and alpha sprang to mind.

She didn't understand what it was about the big guy that made her ache, only that he did. He was the total opposite of her normal type, too, when she'd had a type. Then again, look at how that had ended up. Maybe she needed a man who was the opposite of what she normally went for, and this remote ranch was a place where she could explore that.

Not that she had seen Duncan this past week.

A big, black German Shepard bounded up to her out of nowhere. She yelped and put her hands up defensively as he charged toward her.

A sharp whistle echoed in the cabin. The dog halted on a dime, plopped his butt down on the hardwood flooring, and grinned up at her, with his tongue lolling out and a smile on his face.

"What the fuck are you doing here?" The deep, masculine growl made Eve quake, but not in fear as her head shot up and she spied the man she had been fantasizing about seconds before.

He scowled as he stalked toward her. His long legs ate up the distance in no time. Self-preservation had her retreating until she found herself with her back pressed up against the armoire that held all the sex toys and condoms.

She shivered when he stopped a foot from her. His dark glower would have made her pee her pants if she hadn't already gone.

Duncan looked like he wanted to thrash her—or take a bite out of her.

In a short, clipped voice, he muttered, "I'm going to ask you again. What the hell are you doing in here?"

"I needed to go to the bathroom; thought it was a guest cabin. I knocked first and no one answered, but when I tried the door, it was unlocked. I meant no harm. Truly."

"This isn't a guest cabin."

No. No, it was not. It was a sex cabin. She swallowed the lump in her throat and whispered, "I can see that now."

"What's your endgame here? Why are you at Silver Springs Ranch?" he snarled, leaning in, crowding her against the armoire. He was so close, she could feel the heat pumping off his form. Smell his deep, unique masculine scent that was all him, and better than any cologne. She wanted to plant her face in his chest and inhale him, surround herself with his essence.

"That's no concern of yours," she replied, plastered against the wood, calling herself a fool for wanting him, for wanting to give in to the yearning he engendered.

"It is when it comes to the people I consider my family." His face darkened and turned downright menacing. He backed her up further until there was only a sliver of space between their bodies. His face was mere inches from hers. It should have scared her. But she felt like she was standing on this precipice of need, and all it would take was a small push to send her leaping over the edge.

Her gaze darted to his lips—those full, sensual lips shrouded by an inky close-cropped beard. His warm breath washed over her face. She wet her dry lips, and lifted her gaze up to her tormentor until she was staring into his dark eyes.

The anger that had been present moments before had shifted. She quivered at the sudden hungry flames burning in those black eyes, which rattled her to her core.

Duncan wanted her, as astonishing as it seemed, and her insides turned liquid at the thought of feeling him against her.

When she didn't back away, he leaned in, testing, like he was wondering if she would pull away.

The truth was her limbs were leaden, rooting her feet to the floor. It would take someone dynamiting her out of the spot to get her to move.

She couldn't explain her actions, except, she was tired. So damn tired of being alone, of running, of keeping herself apart from people out of fear. When all he seemed to make her want to do was lean into him, absorb some of his strength and not have to worry for a damn minute. She yearned to feel something other than fear and that, combined with a healthy dose of curiosity about the taciturn alpha, meant she found herself leaning in, meeting him halfway. His nostrils flared and his gaze darkened with desire when he realized her intent.

Eve pressed her mouth against his, just a simple touch really, but one she felt to the soles of her feet. She kissed him hesitantly, exploring his firm lips. On a groan, his hands bracketed her face. He shifted the angle of the kiss and delved deeply, plunging inside, tangling their tongues together in a kiss that left her moaning and clinging to him.

Plastered against him, she felt every hard line of his warrior's body. He dominated the exchange. He kissed her so deeply, it felt like he was a part of her. Until this moment, Eve hadn't understood the term *ravish*. But she did now. Because it was exactly what Duncan was doing with his lips slanted over hers.

Her breath came from him as he ate at her mouth, sucking and nipping her bottom lip before diving even deeper into the miasma of desire. Her nails dug into his chest.

She was melting. Her insides turned into a heated mass of energy. Her sex throbbed in agony. Need battered her defenses.

She was his to command. Until now, she had never truly been kissed—they had all been pale imitations.

One of his hands slid down her back and cupped her bottom, squeezing and pulling her even closer so that she felt the proof of his desire. He brought her leg up around his waist. She lifted the other one of her own accord.

His dark, sexy groan at the intimate contact added to the heat flooding her veins.

This was what she wanted, what she needed. All her worries slid away as he kissed her. In this moment, nothing else mattered, not her job, not that she had an ex-con stalking her across the country, nor that she had been forced to change her name and leave behind everything she had ever known. All that mattered was that he kept on kissing her brainless.

Knocking his ballcap off, she fisted her hands in his hair, trapping his mouth against hers, returning his kiss as he ground his pelvis against hers. And holy smokes, she wanted his hands on her, wanted to run her palms over his firm chest, feel him glide inside her.

A cold, wet nose pressed between them. One minute, she was enmeshed in this erotic, sexual frenzy and in the next, the cold, wet dog nose acted like a bucket of ice water being dumped over their heads.

She tore her mouth from his, and shoved at his chest. Duncan stared at her, breathing heavily as she tried to put distance between them.

What the hell had she been thinking?

Slowly, he set her back on her feet before taking a step back and then another. He reached down and picked up his ballcap from the floor, never taking his eyes off her.

"I should go," she whispered, her body vibrating with such potent need, her knees were still weak.

"I'll drive you home."

"You don't—"

"Don't argue, Eve. The sun is already setting and you're small enough that you'd be a tasty snack for a hungry mountain lion."

She bit back a retort at the mulish expression on his face. She nodded. "Fine."

Brushing past him, she strode out of the cabin without a backward glance. As aroused as she was, if she looked at him, she would jump his bones. And she doubted that was a good idea. Much like eating an entire pint of ice cream, if she gave in, she would most likely regret it. A moment of passion wasn't worth the headache sleeping with Duncan could cause. She needed the job more than she needed sex.

Right?

The big dog kept getting in her way as she marched toward his truck.

"Sampson, get in the back, you rascal," Duncan ordered, and she heard him slam the cabin door shut behind her with a firm thud. "It's unlocked."

She nodded and climbed into the passenger seat of the large dark gray truck. The vehicle smelled like him. Her lips were still swollen from that kiss. And she could taste him.

She kept her mouth shut and stared out the passenger side window. Need chugged through her veins, but she refused to give in to it. If she glanced his way, she couldn't be certain that she could keep her hands to herself.

They drove in silence. The tension was so thick, it was suffocating.

She had never felt this relieved to see her stupid cabin. He pulled up and parked right in front. In a flash, she had her seatbelt off and was climbing out of the cab.

"Thank you." She shot him a quick glance.

In the darkening twilight, he stared, those dark eyes liquid pools of night. "Have a good night. No more trespassing where you don't belong."

She nodded. "I wasn't trying to... never mind."

Furious with herself, with him, with the whole damn

world and state of her life, she slammed the door shut and stomped up the stairs to her front door. It was ridiculous that she was letting him have this much influence over her emotions. It had been an honest mistake.

Duncan stayed in the driveway until she'd entered the cabin and shut the door behind her. And if she closed the door with more force than necessary, so be it.

She was making brownies for dinner, hoping that the deluge of fudgy goodness would dilute the need still humming in her veins.

Because if not, she would do something extremely dumb, like get in her truck and go from cabin to cabin until she located Duncan's vehicle so they could pick up where they'd left off at the sex cabin.

And that would be the most reckless thing she had done in ages.

7

With her paycheck burning a hole in her pocket, the moment Eve clocked out at three on Friday afternoon, she headed into town. The local grocery store customer service department cashed paychecks—for a small fee, of course. But it kept her from needing to open a bank account with false information.

That was one of the things she had been forced to figure out over the last year. Especially given how many times she had changed her name. Each time she had been forced to run, she'd contacted the dealer she had met in the first town she had escaped to, and had him create an entirely new set of identification for her. Over the last year, she had been Peggy Clark, Jennifer Owens, Alyssa Johnson, Molly Burke and, finally, Eve Carruthers.

That had been one of her bus stops when she had zigzagged her way across the country trying to lose Trevor once again—picking up the driver's license, social security card, and passport for Eve Carruthers.

And for now, if anyone asked why she didn't set up a

checking account, she would lie and say she wanted to make sure that the job worked out before she committed to doing something of that nature. It was a valid excuse.

Behind the counter was a friendly face, one she had begun to be familiar with. Beth was a blonde mother of three who worked behind the counter at Kriegel's Grocery store forty hours a week while her husband worked at one of the local ski lodges.

"Well, hello again. Eve, isn't it?" Beth commented with a pretty smile.

"Hi Beth. It's kind of you to remember me."

"What can I do for you today?" Beth asked, her face beaming. She had the perfect personality for customer service.

"I would like to cash my paycheck, if that's all right. I know there's a fee for it."

"Sure thing." Beth took the check and Eve's fake Louisiana driver's license, and began entering the information into her register. "You know, hon, it would be cheaper for you to open an account over at the bank."

"I know, but until I'm one hundred percent certain the position over at Silver Springs Ranch is going to work out, I would rather not open something that I will just have to close a month or so later."

"I hear you. It's a lot of paperwork and hassle if that's the case," Beth said, counting out the full amount of Eve's paycheck minus the fee: all five hundred and sixty-eight dollars.

It was enough that she could start filling the pantry and purchasing the supplies she needed, like some winter boots that wouldn't leave her slipping and sliding all over the place.

"Is that all you needed today, hon?"

"Yep. I'll be back in a bit to get my groceries. I have a few other stops I need to make first, though."

"Well, if I'm gone for the day by the time you get back, have a great weekend."

"You too, Beth."

Eve headed out of the grocery store. She decided to keep her truck parked in the grocery store lot and walk to the shoe store. At Bucky's shoe store, she found a sturdy pair of snow boots that were half off on a holiday sale. Thank you, Christmas!

She had saved enough on the boots that she was able to head over to the outdoor supply store, and find a much better, thicker coat that would keep her warm during the winter months at the ranch. She also grabbed a hat, some gloves, and scarf. She had the sales lady remove all the tags at the register so she could put her new coat and hat on.

Feeling like she was starting to chisel her way down her list of things she needed to purchase, she walked the few blocks back to her truck and stored the purchases she wasn't wearing in the front cab. Then she headed back into the grocery store.

On a mission to bulk up her supplies, she picked up cans of beans and corn, as well as frozen packs of veggies and frozen meals to stock her freezer with. She bought extra coffee, coffee filters, and creamer, selected multiple packs of meat, beef, pork, and chicken, grabbed an extra carton of eggs, and got bacon, cheese, fresh fruit and veggies.

Then she ended up in the baking supplies aisle and went a little crazy. She had a hankering for some cranberry orange muffins and lemon poppy seed bread. Going a little overboard, she almost wiped out the rest of her paycheck at the checkout counter. But then, she needed a whisk, rolling pin, and a few other implements that the cabin wasn't already stocked with. Who could blame her?

This was the first time in a year she felt like she was living in a place she could make permanent. Which was why she decided that if she had extra, she would take a loaf to Amber on Monday, kind of as a thank you for the job.

Besides, she was paid weekly and had cash left over from last week that she had hidden in the lockbox she stored beneath her bed. While she hated the cliché of keeping money tucked beneath her bed, that was where it was safest if she had to bolt in a hurry.

One of the life lessons she had learned on the run.

Eve carted her purchases out to her truck, rather pleased with her haul. She'd bought enough that she had to put a few bags in the bed of the truck. If she was at Silver Springs Ranch long enough, she might want to consider getting one of those locking covers installed on the truck bed. It was something to think about and consider if she was going to be here for the long haul.

Living on and working at the ranch long term opened up a boatload of possibilities. She might be able to date. And while she couldn't commit in a legal way, given the documents she would end up falsifying, that didn't mean she couldn't date and have sex.

As she pulled out of her parking space, it was Duncan's image that blossomed in her mind. The way he had looked at her with lust turning his eyes black, panting from their torridly hot kiss.

She rubbed her fingers over her mouth. She could still feel him at the oddest times, like now. When she thought about sex, it inevitably made her think of him. The two seemed to go hand in hand. And she wondered, on more than one occasion, if he ever went to the sex dungeon cabin.

Eve didn't understand why the thought of it, of him, turned her on. She only knew that it did—so much so that she had thought of little else over the past week. Even though she hadn't seen him at all this past week, he had starred in more than a few of her fantasies.

It had been longer than she would like to admit since she had done the horizontal tango with anyone. But when that fateful night had happened a year ago, she had already been on an eighteen month dry spell, since none of the guys she'd attempted to date had made it past the three date benchmark.

Then the night with Trevor had happened, and being on the run, looking over her shoulder constantly, hadn't put her in the mood to flirt with any of the men she had met, much to their chagrin. And not for lack of trying on their parts.

But the thing was, when you were focused on survival, dating and sex took a back seat to everything else.

She glanced in her rearview mirror and realized the truck that had pulled out behind her after she left the grocery store parking lot was still behind her. She sped up a little, just by a few miles per hour, to see if she could lose them. She didn't like to speed too much out of fear that she would get pulled over, and tossed in jail for her false identification.

The truck didn't speed up. She released the breath she had been holding and maintained the slightly faster speed. Along the two-lane highway, she kept glancing in her rearview mirror. The truck didn't turn off, speed up, or slow down. It maintained its present heading and course—tailing her.

She told herself it was nothing to be concerned about. There was no way—with all the crisscrossing she had done—that Trevor could have found her this quickly.

But even as she had that thought, her heart pounded wildly in her chest at the truck pacing her. Fear beat a solid, sure drumbeat in her veins and twisted her stomach up in knots.

At the entrance to Silver Springs Ranch, she took the left turn off the highway. Glancing in her rearview mirror as she entered the ranch property, she sucked in a swift breath when she saw the truck make the same turn.

It was most likely a tourist, or one of the workers. She would see how, in a minute, they would take one of the many offshoots from the main road, and she would know there was nothing to be worried about.

She took the right onto the road that led to her cabin. Staring in the mirror, she whimpered when the truck behind her made the same turn.

Trying not to panic and to maintain a level head, she tried to think about what steps she should take. Was it Trevor? Was she that idiotic to believe he wouldn't find her this swiftly when he had located her every other time?

Should she loop back around and go to the main hotel? The very last thing she would do was lead him straight to her cabin. It made her want to cry to think she would have to ditch the baking gadgets she'd picked up at the store. It was a small thing when compared with getting to live another day, but it still made her want to weep.

She was so damn tired of running, of being afraid, of being alive but not being able to live.

What kind of life was this?

After the first half mile, the truck was still following her. She made a split decision, and whipped the truck over onto the shoulder. She would let them pass her. Then she would turn around, head to the hotel, and be around other people before making the trek home.

She almost peed her pants when the truck pulled up behind hers.

Making sure the doors were locked, she gripped the steering wheel tight as a big man disembarked from the truck cab. In the darkening twilight, she couldn't make out his features. The headlights only emphasized his bigger size.

With her heart racing like a jackrabbit, she cursed herself for not bringing her gun with her. She hadn't thought to bring it, and that was the problem. She didn't think. She was still the unsuspecting woman who thought everyone was honest and trustworthy, when that wasn't the case at all.

Heart hammering, she kept the truck in drive with her foot on the brake as the man approached. She figured she needed to know if it was Trevor or not. If it was him, she would bolt. Go find a place to hide for a few hours before heading to the cabin to retrieve her meager belongs and hit the road. With the truck, she could head west or east, or wherever she thought she could lose him again.

The man made it to her door and knocked on the window.

Saying a silent prayer, she glanced out at him. Her breath expelled in a rush.

It wasn't Trevor.

But she did recognize the man.

"Is everything all right? It's Eve, right?" The man wore a black Stetson on top of his head which blended with his black hair and beard. He had a kind smile on his face.

She rolled her window down an inch. "Yes, I'm fine. Thank you."

"I didn't mean to scare you. I was just worried something was wrong when you pulled off like that. And I thought it was a fine opportunity for me to tell you that one of your rear brake lights is out."

"Oh. Thank you. I had no idea."

"If you'd like, I can fix it for you. I've got your chimney on my maintenance list this week—to fix that faulty flue valve. It would be a quick and easy thing for me to replace for you."

"Oh, that would be nice. But I'll have my truck at the hotel."

"It's no bother. That's where I start my days at, anyhow. I can find it in the employee lot and install a new bulb for you."

"That would be really appreciated... ah, I'm sorry, but I don't remember your name." She smiled.

"It's Lincoln. I'm head of maintenance for the ranch."

"Lincoln, right. Sorry, there are so many people on this ranch and I'm horrible at remembering names," she replied, the smile still tight on her face.

"No worries. We just met the once. Is there anything else at the cabin that needs fixing?"

"Um, not that I know of right now."

"Well, if something comes up before Wednesday, just write it down and leave the note on the fireplace, and I will get to it."

"That's great. Thanks."

He tipped his hat. "It was good to see you again, Eve. I'm around if you need anything. You have a good night now."

"You too." She waved him off, then pressed a hand to her heart.

Holy shit!

She needed chocolate and wine stat after that scare. Before Lincoln made it back into his truck, she pulled away and drove the remaining two miles to her cabin, berating herself the entire drive. His truck once again followed behind hers but now that she knew definitively it wasn't Trevor, she could relax.

When she pulled into the driveway of her cabin, he honked as he passed her by.

There were a number of things she had done wrong this afternoon. First, she had let her guard down. That was a surefire way to end up dead. And second, she had allowed her mind to wander when she should have remained vigilant. It was one thing to be woolgathering at home, quite another when she was out in public. Third, she'd left her weapon at home. She did that because she wasn't trained on the stupid thing, and worried about accidentally hurting someone. Well, no more. If there was anything this instance had taught her, it was that she needed to get trained on the damn thing. And anytime she left the house, she needed to have the gun on her.

She might want to look and see if there was a shooting range in town where she could go and get herself taught. Or perhaps one of the cowboys on the ranch could teach her—like that Lincoln, he seemed nice enough.

But he wouldn't be the best person for the job, she thought as she set her purchases on the kitchen counter. She knew the man who was the best suited. The man who had been trained to be a total badass. The one who had kissed her brainless in ten seconds flat.

Duncan.

Would he even consider training her on the firearm? He seemed to be avoiding her since their last interaction.

But perhaps she needed more than just training on the firearm. She needed to learn self-defense, and how to fight back. She had never thrown a punch in her life, other than her fist to Trevor's eye. And that instance was something that replayed in her nightmares on a recorded loop when she was super stressed.

She'd give it some more thought before deciding on whether to approach Duncan or not. Because the truth was, she didn't know if she could be around him and not want him. Letting her guard down that much could prove to be fatal.

---

8

*A*fter a three day camping trip, all Duncan wanted was a shower, a hot meal, a beer, and a willing woman. He'd settle for three out of four. Especially considering whenever he thought about a willing woman, Eve's visage came to mind—the way she had looked in Cabin X after their unexpected lip lock. Her lips had been swollen, her golden gaze liquid with desire, and it had taken every ounce of strength he possessed not to press forward, see if he could convince her to let him take her to bed.

Christ, she had starred in his fantasies the past week. And he had taken to driving by her cabin on his way into the hotel to prep for another camping trip. He'd been rather startled to see her lights on at four in the morning, or late at night when he was returning from a night at the Bucking Bronco. He had avoided going to Park Tavern because as much as he liked Maribella, he wasn't in the mood for her pouting when he turned her down. Now that he had a taste for Eve, she had become an obsession.

The mixture of fierceness and fragility, combined with the explosive passion he had found in her arms, was an intoxicating addiction. The woman was dangerous to his sense of wellbeing, but like an addict, he didn't care. Which was why he had taken great pains not to cross paths with her this past week. Given that they both lived and worked on the ranch, it was difficult, but not impossible.

After his shower, he fed Sampson, who thankfully on this trip had not rolled in bear shit or fish guts. Hopefully, the knucklehead was learning, since he tended to view baths as torture. Not that Duncan had any real faith in that thought. The silly pup loved nothing more than getting into things he shouldn't.

Duncan stood at his fridge in a pair of sweats with a beer in his hand and contemplated the frozen pizza in his freezer as a possible option. It wasn't Mrs. Gregory's cooking but then nothing else was, and the frozen supreme pizza was still better than the MREs he had eaten in the Navy. He'd just reached up to withdraw the package when there was a knock on his door.

He glanced at the time on the microwave.

Eight at night on a Sunday, who the hell was paying him a call tonight? Most people didn't know his schedule since it varied so much week to week, other than Matt, Eli, or Amber.

Shutting the freezer, he set his beer on the counter and plodded over to the front door where Sampson already stood, his tail wagging at the prospect of company. Duncan flipped the lock and yanked the door open.

Eve?

Shock filled him. She was the last person he'd expected to find. How had she known where to find him? It wasn't like his name was on the mailbox. She stared at him with a tremulous smile, her hands clenched, skittishly shifting on her feet. But it was the haunted look in her eyes that pierced him like an arrow straight through his chest. Whatever she had seen in her life had been bad, and it ate at her.

He understood the feeling well. Because there were some things which never went away, no matter how much one tried to expel them from their psyche. All you could do was compartmentalize it, lock it away out of sight, and hope that it would leave you in peace.

"Eve. What can I do for you?" he asked, more than curious about her unexpected visit.

"I'm sorry to bother you. This was a stupid idea. Never mind." She shook her head and started to back away.

He grabbed her wrist. She flinched, and then acted as if nothing happened, schooling her features into a pleasant smile.

Oh, baby. Someone hurt you really bad, didn't they?

He tugged her inside and shut the door, then drew her over into the living room, watching her gaze dart around the place almost like she was looking for monsters. Her puffy gray coat dwarfed her body. The ivory beanie on her head stood out in stark contrast to the long inky hair that fell past her shoulders. And he couldn't even look further south at her legs in those jeans, because he remembered how they had fit around his waist.

"Tell me what's going on." He shifted, using the dominant tone he utilized with a woman during a scene.

"Okay, well, the thing is," she started babbling, twisting her hands together nervously, "that I know you were right the other day. After a silly incident where I thought I was being followed, I realized that I need to learn. And it got me thinking about what I need to do."

He was confused by her babbling. The nerves were pumping off her in waves. Having her there, in his place as she stood there fidgeting, he was struck again. She really was a small thing, with birdlike bones.

"Why are you here?" His stomach clenched. Because, dammit, he knew what he wished she was here for—to pick up exactly where they had left off a week ago. She might be a mess, but she was a hot mess he wouldn't mind taking to his bed, not after tasting the wildness, the hunger, and passion in her.

"You were in the military, right?"

"Yes. I was a Navy SEAL. Why?"

"I need to learn how to defend myself. I know you don't like me very much. But I was hoping that you would set that aside and teach me," she pleaded, looking at him like he was her savior.

He rocked back on his heels. Shock riddled him. Whatever she was running from, it was something that made her scared enough to come to him for aid. It perversely pleased him, though. As a Dominant and a former Naval officer, he couldn't turn away from a woman in need. The wheels turned. If he trained her, they would end up spending a lot of time together one on one.

Perhaps, if he agreed, he could end up training her in another fashion. Expel his obsession with her by gorging on her slim form for a few nights. He never took it further than that with a woman, anyway. And while she was an employee at the ranch, there was no written rule that said employees couldn't fraternize with each other—although it was likely frowned upon.

She shook her head. "This was stupid. I'm sorry for bothering you. I'll just—"

"Sit. Down."

She froze at his command, then glanced at the leather chair and took a seat without putting up a protest. The speed with which she responded made him wonder if she might be submissive. The thought of that, of having her submit to him, of restraining her on one of the many pieces of BDSM furniture in Cabin X, made him hard as a fucking rock.

Sampson sat beside the chair she was in and put his head on the chair arm with a hopeful glance at her. The silly pup loved people and Eve had garnered his attention —much like she had his owner.

Duncan sat facing her on the sofa, hoping like hell she didn't notice his hard on. "What are you wanting to learn? Just hand to hand self-defense?"

It was rather curious. Since leaving the Navy, he'd never had anyone approach him to train them to fight or to defend themselves.

"Self-defense... and how to shoot a firearm. My firearm, to be precise."

He narrowed his eyes. "The hand to hand is no problem. We can start that tomorrow night, here at my place. But if I'm going to put a gun in your hands and teach you to shoot, you're going to have to tell me why you want to learn."

Eve turned mulish and defensive. "Why do you need to know that?"

"Because, if I'm teaching you the proper way to shoot a gun, I need to know that you aren't planning on heading to your last employer and racking up mass casualties. I've got enough blood on my hands after twelve years of service. I don't need more."

"Oh no, nothing like that. It's purely for self-defense. Since I bought the gun a few months back, I just haven't had the time to get properly trained. And like you mentioned, before I go and pick it up again, I should know the right way to handle it."

Duncan assessed her. There was more she wasn't telling him. He knew it just as surely as he knew the sun would rise in the morning.

"We'll start with the self-defense training first. Until I know you can handle yourself in that fashion, I won't be putting a gun in your hands."

"But—"

"That's nonnegotiable, honey. If you want my help, want me to train you, then we're doing it my way, not yours. Take it or leave it." He wanted her to say yes, dammit. Which meant he had gone completely mental.

She stared at him, chewing on her plump bottom lip. It shouldn't turn him on. But it made him want to pick her up and carry her into his bedroom for some training of a different variety.

"Okay, I agree." She held out her hand for him to shake.

Victory raced through him. He would train her. Push her buttons, and see if he could get her into his bed as well. Closing his hand around her much smaller one as they sealed their pact, he said, "We begin tomorrow night. Be here at seven sharp. I can give you two hours."

She smiled then, a genuine, pure smile that quite simply took his breath away. Eve was fucking gorgeous. He was going to enjoy peeling her layers away. He planned to uncover why she felt she needed to defend herself. That would come as she trusted him more.

"Thank you." She withdrew her hand with a slight blush creeping into her cheeks.

"Wear comfortable clothes that you can move in."

"Okay. Anything else?"

"Come prepared to learn. You will learn what I decide you need. Understood?"

She nodded. "Absolutely. You don't know how much I appreciate this, Duncan. Truly. I've interrupted your evening. I won't keep you any longer."

Eve rose—more like shot up—full of nerves once more.

"It wasn't any bother." He escorted her to the door with a palm on her lower back, noting that she didn't move away from his touch. After their kiss last week, he'd worried that he had somehow misread the signals.

At the door, she turned and smiled up at him. When her gaze dropped to his lips, he couldn't help but smile.

Oh yeah, the game had changed between them. And while she did present some danger to his status as an eternal bachelor, he tended to be an adrenaline junkie— or he had been, otherwise he never would have survived as a SEAL.

But this challenge would be far more enticing than any mission he'd ever engaged in.

"Good night," she murmured.

"Sweet dreams. I'll see you tomorrow."

"Tomorrow," she said, then sailed out of his door. He and Sampson stood watching her get into her truck and start it. He didn't close the door until she had backed out of his drive and driven off.

Well hell, didn't that beat all? And he had to admit it was the most fascinating thing to happen to him since he had left the service.

9

From the outside, Duncan's cabin looked like the rest of them on the ranch, a rustic log cabin with a sizable porch. But this one also had a shed off to the side and his big, dark gray truck parked out front. And inside was a man full of danger and secrets who, for whatever reason, had kissed her—a kiss with more passion than she had experienced with any other man. Not that there was a long list of them. There had been too much responsibility on her shoulders after her parents died.

On the short trek from her truck to his front door, Eve wiped her sweaty palms on her yoga pants. It was ridiculous that she was nervous about tonight.

Just because they had kissed once didn't mean that they would do it again.

The real question was: did she want to kiss him? Yes. No. She didn't know.

She shouldn't want to kiss him. She should want to keep herself on emotional lockdown like she had over the past year. It was far simpler if she didn't get attached to anyone since inevitably, she would be forced to move on.

But what if she didn't have to leave? What if this could be the place where she made her stand and stopped running?

Because if that was the case, if she was brave enough to face the bane of her existence, then she wanted all the kisses from Duncan. All of them. Every lip smacking, earth shattering, kiss that left her in a melted puddle at his impressively large feet.

Chewing on her bottom lip, she knocked on his front door.

Eve wasn't certain what she expected, but it wasn't Duncan in a pair of gray basketball shorts and a white tee shirt that clung to every single one of his rock hard muscles. A bolt of kinetic energy struck her form and left her midsection quivering... in tingling anticipation. Even his calves were sexy as hell.

"Come in, Eve."

Duncan stared in an assessing, piercing fashion that always unnerved her but tonight it made her skin feel three sizes too small.

"Um, hi. I appreciate you doing this." She entered his house, telling herself this was the right move on her part.

Sampson, the big German Shephard, stood right inside the door with his tail furiously wagging. He approached with his tongue hanging out in a friendly, *how do you do, so excited to see you*, smile.

She held her hand out for him to sniff, and got a big, sloppy wet kiss on her palm.

"You're just a big baby, aren't you?" She scratched

behind his ears. Maybe that was something she needed, too: a big, scary dog like Sampson to offer a measure of protection. It was something to think about, at the very least.

Loving the attention, Sampson jumped up, putting his paws on against her shoulders. She wasn't expecting the dog to throw his full weight against her in his exuberance. She stumbled back.

But Duncan was there. He came up behind her and caught her before she fell to the ground.

"Whoa there. Get down, bud, we don't jump on guests." He held her with one hand and shoved Sampson off her. With his body up against hers, he asked, "You all right? He's harmless."

"Yes. I'm fine. It's no bother. He just startled me, is all."

"I can put him in the bedroom while you're here, that way, he won't bother you." He hadn't moved away from her yet, sending her heart racing.

"Oh, don't do that. It's not a big deal, really. I'm fine. This is his home. He shouldn't have to get locked up because I'm here."

"If you're sure."

"I am." She nodded and took a deep breath as he finally released her.

He ushered her into the living room, where he had pushed his big sofa and coffee table out of the way. "Have you had any kind of self-defense training at all?"

She winced and shook her head. "No."

"Not even a boxing or Tae Kwon Do class?"

She laid her purse and coat on the sofa. "No. None of that."

"Then we'll be starting with the basics first before we get to the defense part of your training. Hold your dominant hand out and ball your fist up for me."

She did as he asked without question. Holding her right hand out, she curled her fingers into a fist.

"If you throw a punch with your hand like that, you'll break your thumb." He took her hand between his much larger ones, and moved her thumb from its position at the side of her fingers.

"You want your thumb to cover the middle knuckle of your first two fingers, like this. Using this form will help keep you from injuring your thumb or wrist. Understand?"

"Yes." It felt strange to hold her hand in that position, unnatural even, but she did it. She was determined more than ever to fight back the next time Trevor came for her.

"Good. Now, I want you to punch my palm with your fist. Let me see what you think a punch is so I can see what I'm working with." He held up both hands, his gaze steady on her.

Focusing on his palm and not his face, because she couldn't seem to concentrate when she looked at his face, she pulled back and struck his palm, then grimaced when she didn't even make his palm waver in the slightest.

Before she drew her fist back, he closed his hand around hers. "The first rule of self-defense, Eve, is when you're out of your depth, when your opponent is bigger and stronger, run. It will keep you alive to fight again."

Running was something she knew how to do, and do

well. She glanced at him then. "And if I can't run? If I'm trapped, and..." She couldn't even go there, back to that night. The horror of it was emblazoned across her soul.

Understanding filled his gaze. "That's what we're going to work on, getting you out of those tight spots. But I want you to remember that running should be your first objective. There's no shame in running."

"What do you know about running?" The guy was solidly built and a total badass. It was in the way he carried himself. "You don't seem like there's anything you fear."

"Then you're not really looking. Every man, every person, fears something. You just have to decide whether you are going to let that fear control you, or you control it. And I've run from my fair share of fights. Because if you're smart, you only fight when you must, otherwise you run."

Shadows danced across his gaze. It was then she saw the war hardened, battle weary soldier beneath the tough exterior. In his solemn stare was a man who had seen things that would make most people crumble and yet he was still standing, still surviving. He could have let his experiences make him a bitter asshole, but he hadn't. Moody and a bit taciturn, to be sure, but he was a good man.

"I don't want it to control me," she whispered. This was her trying to take back her life, and live.

A slow smile spread over his face, making her breath catch in her throat. "Good. Now we will really begin your training."

He took her through the proper way to throw a

punch until she was sweating and panting. And Duncan wasn't even breathing heavily. Bastard. Over the past year, she hadn't realized how out of shape she had become. Since she'd gone on the run, her daily workouts had vanished from her life, and it showed.

"Okay, now we're going to move on to heel strikes. These are good for disabling your opponent swiftly so that you can get away to safety. Again, with your dominant hand, flex your hand up like this and keep your palm open." He held his hand up. "And then you aim for either their nose or throat. You want to jab upwards, aiming for their nostrils or their throat."

He demonstrated the move. She could watch him all day long, she realized. There was a beauty and fluidity to his movements, his control and command of his body.

"Now, you want to make sure when you strike that, you go hard and fast, making sure to recoil your arm back quickly. If you do it right, it should snap your opponent's head up and back. I want you to try it on me."

She nibbled on her bottom lip. "Are you sure? I don't want to hurt you."

He chuckled. "Honey, I'll be fine. Now do it."

He lifted his hand and gestured for her to take a shot at him. His response was like a pat on the head that she was a good, weak little girl, incapable of taking him out. And yeah, she realized that he was an elite former military soldier.

But it still fucking pissed her off.

Before her brain could tell her not to, she drew her arm back, opened her palm just like he had shown her, and went for his jugular. She was so damn tired of being seen as weak.

Her palm cracked against his chin, and snapped his head back.

With her palm throbbing, she froze with her jaw wide open. She sputtered, "I'm so sorry. Are you okay?"

He leveled her with a grin, pride shining in his dark gaze. "Now you're talking. That was a good hit. Try it again. Use whatever it was that fueled that hit. I want you to focus on your form. And remember, keep your eyes on me. Don't ever take them off your opponent."

The unexpected praise washed over her like a warm ocean wave. Settling in as confidence swam through her chest, she did as he asked, performing the open-palmed punch again and again.

But she only got him that once.

"Okay, those are both good moves if you have the space. If it's close quarters and there's not enough room for you to properly strike your opponent with a punch, then use your elbows. If you're in a situation where you are being attacked, you have just seconds to disarm the attacker, injure them enough to get away. I'm going to crowd you, give you no option but to come at me with an elbow strike." He performed the movement a couple times. His powerfully built form rippled with muscles as he moved, distracting her as he approached. "Ready?"

"Um, yep." Heat pinged low in her stomach as he neared. It was one thing to be dancing and moving around him, keeping him at arm's length. But being this close brought up memories from the other night of their one and only kiss.

She couldn't help remembering it, either, which was beyond frustrating.

Because for all the issues she had about trusting men, where Duncan was concerned, she didn't doubt him. Not when she saw him, the steady confidence, the tireless work ethic, the kindness and affection he showed his dog —and even her after their ignoble first few interactions— and all of it was enshrined with a layer of honor that he would do the right thing all the time, every time.

It made him trustworthy.

That, combined with the fact that he was sinfully sexy and could kiss her blind in seconds, made him undeniably the most potent male of her acquaintance.

He danced out of the way. The guy was surprisingly light on his feet for such a large man. But then he moved like lightning, trapping her back up against his body. His arm closed around her chest like a leaded weight. The air exploded from her lungs as she gripped his arm.

"This is why you need to strike hard and fast, then run, in any type of attack. Once they grab you and bind your hands, you're done. I want you to try using your elbow and striking it back as hard as you can," he murmured beside her ear.

Her heart pounded a quick tempo at feeling his solid two hundred pounds of muscle aligned against her body. It took every ounce of concentration she possessed to focus on the task at hand, and not on the way she was incinerating from the inside out.

He held her firmly while she struggled to try and use her dominant arm for an elbow jab to his midsection.

"Come on. Again. Use your instinct and think as you

work to free yourself. In a situation like this, speed and force are key."

Gritting her teeth, she slammed her elbow into his ribs. He hissed. His hold slackened.

Eve glanced up over her shoulder at him. She laid her hand over his cheek. "Are you all right?"

He stilled against her. His gaze turned downright incendiary.

Unable to refrain any longer, proceeding on instinct with desire pumping through her body after being held and surrounded by him, she pressed her mouth over his, sucking his bottom lip into her mouth.

Duncan's lips were soft as silk for a man who spent the bulk of his life outdoors. That contradiction left her sighing, pressing deeper as she kissed him.

Duncan's low groan made everything inside her tighten and quiver.

She turned in to him, shifting as he assumed command, until she was flush against his hard form. She clung to him, her hands sliding up his chest, marveling at the lack of give in his muscles, only to creep up around his neck and bury her hands in his hair. She gripped him tight as his silken tongue stroked and plunged inside her mouth, tangling with hers in a carnal dance that left her whimpering.

Those big hands of his caressed her slowly, from her shoulders along her spine. He left a trail of flames and shivering need behind on his journey south.

Lust pulsed in her loins, turning her sex buttery, greedy to feel him inside.

She never knew she could be kissed this way, like he

would die if he didn't taste her. He sucked and bit her bottom lip before changing the angle and sealing his mouth over hers.

A hand cupped her breast through the fabric of her shirt and sports bra. Her nipple hardened at his touch, pinging a rush of pleasure through her body to coalesce in her core. Warning bells sounded in her head.

Panic slammed into her. She shoved at his chest, ripped her mouth from his and pleaded breathily, "Stop."

Duncan stilled, and narrowed his gaze. With his jaw tightly clenched, he lifted his hands from her form.

The moment he did, she retreated a few steps.

"Don't do that again unless you plan to finish what you start."

She noticed the firm bulge beneath his pants. God, he was big in every way. And for a moment, she warred with herself on whether to reach out and resume where she had stopped them. She panted, wanting him, wishing she was brave enough to take what she wanted, but those warning signals blared in her psyche.

"I'm sorry. I didn't mean..." She shook her head, fighting back tears as embarrassment flooded her.

She was an idiot. He had been kind, gone out of his way to help her, and how did she repay him? By groping and kissing him, only to shut it down the moment it went too far because she was afraid. Not of him, but of herself, and her response to him.

"I think we're done tonight. You did well. We can resume when I return."

Her head shot up. "You're leaving?"

"I have a three-night camping trip to oversee, beginning tomorrow. I'll be back Friday. Why don't we plan for Saturday afternoon at one? We'll do another session then."

Instead of berating her or calling her a fool, he was offering to help her out even more. He couldn't be real. She had to be hallucinating. Men were never this helpful.

"Are you sure? I mean... after everything... I would understand if you didn't—"

"Relax, honey, I'm not going to flog you for kissing me. Twice now. Just know, if you do it again, I will finish it and assume you want to spend the night in my bed. So, unless you are one hundred percent certain, don't."

She nodded and slid her coat on, remorse battering her. "Thank you."

Duncan escorted her over to the front door.

At the door, she gazed at him. He wore an unreadable expression. Gone was the hunger or congeniality of the past hour. In their place was a fortress, shielding his emotions and thoughts from her.

He wore his shield as a defense. And even though he smiled, it didn't reach his eyes. There was a sadistic part of her that wanted to needle him, get a rise out of him. It pissed her off that he was this controlled mere moments after one of the hottest kisses of her life, and he acted like it hadn't affected him one bit.

She knew it must be a skill he'd learned in the military, an ability to compartmentalize and shut down his feelings on a dime. She envied him that skill. And for some unknown reason, it pissed her the hell off.

The man before her wasn't the affable man instructing her anymore but the warrior. It was a foundational part of him. He might no longer be serving but he was a soldier, staring down whatever calamity befell him, even when that calamity was her.

"Have a good trip. And thanks again."

Duncan nodded. "Drive safe."

She sailed through his front door with her head held high, trying to keep her cool. Because internally, she felt bipolar, wanting to rage and cry, all at the same time.

It wasn't until she was navigating the small mountain road back to her cabin that she realized her rage had nothing to do with Duncan. It was all self-directed wrath.

Because she wanted him. She wanted him with an intensity and desire that terrified her. He was the first man she had encountered, in the years since her failed relationship with the now-deceased criminal Silas, whom she wanted. He had resurrected her libido, and made her feel things she didn't want to feel. It pissed her off, and left her floundering.

Could she give in, experience the wicked desire in his arms, and not lose herself in him? Would she be able to let him dance with her body when she was lying to him about who she was, and why she was here?

Pulling into her cabin's driveway, she pressed a hand over her heart. No matter the decision she made regarding Duncan, she had to protect her heart.

10

*D*uncan dropped the guests off at reception. The four guys had been celebrating their best bud's impending marriage, and decided a few nights off the grid was the best way to celebrate before they headed to Vegas for the bachelor party.

They had been a good group, more interested at night in drinking beer and swapping stories. Duncan had been forced to rib them considering they had all served in the Air Force and, well, that's what the different branches did: gave each other shit about their military branches. Since he was a SEAL, it had given him the edge.

All in all, it had been one of his more enjoyable camping trips. He had only thought about Eve when he hadn't been focused on the task at hand. But even when he'd focused, he had been hard pressed to keep her from his mind.

In all his life, he had never had a woman affect him the way she did. She had been an eager pupil the other night, listening and following his command without question. Which had led him to ponder what else he could teach her, like how to submit to him body and soul—letting him crack her open and expose all the torrid details of her make up, only to put her back together again.

"Hey Duncan." Jessica gestured him over to the reservation desk.

Sauntering over, wondering what she needed, he asked, "What can I do for you, Jessica?"

"Sorry to do this to you but you've got another trip at noon."

"Really? Matt or Eli aren't available to take them out? How long? And how many in the expedition?"

"They requested you specifically as their guide. There's one in the party, a Ms. Carruthers, and it's a two-night trip."

The last name didn't ring any bells. He shrugged. If the chick wanted him then she would get him. He checked the time on his watch. "I'm running home to shower, change, restock the camping supplies and get something to eat. I'll be back by noon."

"Great. Sorry, but they were insistent that you be their guide and instructor."

He saluted her. "No worries. Be back in a bit."

Duncan headed out to his truck, where Sampson was waiting for him, his head hanging out the window of the back seat. The goofy pup looked like he was having the time of his life.

Duncan drove home. He unpacked the bed of his truck and all the used supplies, storing them right inside the front door. He left Sampson eating a big bowl of dog chow, and headed into the bathroom.

In the shower, he was fast and efficient—at least until his mind veered to Eve and not the tasks he needed to complete over the next hour to make it back to reception in time to pick up his newest camper.

But he couldn't seem to keep his mind off her. Not after the way she had looked in his living room in those black, skin tight yoga pants, the swell of her tits obvious beneath the black sports bra and black tank top she'd worn.

When his dick refused to deflate, he gripped his shaft, stroking the length as he let the fantasy bloom—because, in his fantasies, he had stripped her bare and was feasting on her slim form. He slapped his palm against the tile, bracing himself while he fisted his cock, imagining it was her mouth taking him in, surrounding him.

Then he would push her to the floor on her hands and knees, part the globes of her stellar ass, and plunge the full length inside her hot cunt.

The thought sent him tumbling over the ledge. He tossed back his head beneath the hot spray, coming hard enough that his knees wobbled.

He had been looking forward to seeing her tomorrow.

When had that ever happened? He liked women, enjoyed them immensely, but he never got attached. Yet with Eve, the more time he spent in her company, the more he wanted to spend his free time with her. And she would wind up in his bed, it was only a matter of time.

He didn't even have her phone number to call her

and let her know that he wasn't going to be able to meet her to continue her training.

Shutting the shower off, he figured he could leave a note for her at reception. And then, as soon as he returned home, he was getting her number.

Duncan moved like lightning around his place, dressing in a fresh set of clothes and repacking everything. Since the client was a woman, he would remain aware of her more delicate sensibilities and make sure he didn't start to stink. Granted, he couldn't guarantee that Sampson wouldn't smell. If they came across bear shit, all bets were off.

Duncan packed new supplies of coffee, protein bars, and a few MREs in case fishing was scarce. Double checking his tent and the tent for the ranch guest, he packed everything up in the bed of his truck. Not that there was a lot of gear. On the camping trips, he made sure to take only the essentials, and what could be carried in a backpack.

Also since his client was a woman—not that he doubted their strength—he still loaded his pack with more of the supplies than hers. It was too ingrained in his nature to protect women, remove as much of the burden from their shoulders as possible. And he doubted that would change.

He double checked his firearm was secure, with the safety engaged, and made sure the SAT phone battery was charged. It was enough to see them through to Sunday morning, which was all he cared about.

"Sampson, come on, bud. Let's go." He whistled for the pup.

Sampson eyed him as he climbed down from his spot on the couch. As much as the silly dog enjoyed camping, he loved a good couch nap equally. Not that Duncan could blame him. He could do with a nap himself.

He pulled up in front of the hotel and parked right by the door. It was easier this way, since all he had was one camper.

Outfitted for another woodland trek, he sauntered into the reception desk with the note he planned to leave for Eve at the desk—only to find her standing there.

Her dark hair was braided and fell over one slim shoulder. He assessed her from head to toe, taking in the form-fitting jeans and hiking boots, the turtleneck and sweatshirt with the thick winter coat over it. There was a small backpack at her feet. Sunglasses were hooked into the neck of her shirt.

Jessica chimed, "She's your one camper for this weekend."

Camping... alone... for two days and nights with Eve. Just Eve. "What the hell do you think you're doing?"

He couldn't keep the snarl from his voice. Jessica's brows rose in surprise. But Eve didn't run or seem nervous in the slightest—for a change. If anything, she appeared downright pleased as punch.

"Learning about surviving in the great outdoors. And you?" she asked with a sweet smile, her gaze guarded and unreadable. She normally wore her emotions on her sleeve. This new, unemotional Eve was a damn puzzle, and he felt his ire rising. He didn't know what game she was playing. He clenched his hands to keep himself from grabbing her and shaking some sense into her.

"Why me? There are other guides who are just as skilled. I can't recommend Eli or Matt enough."

"Because I trust you."

There was nothing else the woman could have said that meant more. Her trust in him—when he knew that there was so much more she wasn't saying, that she had been hurt and hurt badly—filled him with unadulterated satisfaction. It was what every Dominant longed to hear from a submissive.

And for her to offer him her trust without reservation wrapped him ever tighter in his need for her. She was his obsession. Now he would have almost forty-eight hours alone with her, to work on her, and see where they landed.

Nodding, he grabbed her pack off the floor. "If you need to use the restroom, this is your last chance for indoor plumbing."

"Ah, right."

"They're around the corner, past the elevator. I'll be at my truck, waiting right outside."

"Okay. Be right out." She hastened away.

The few extra minutes would give him a chance to get his bearings after the shock of finding her at the reservation desk. Back outside, he secured her pack in the truck bed, and made Sampson move into the backseat.

He watched Eve descend the steps. She had added an ivory winter hat and donned her sunglasses. He couldn't help but think she was the most beautiful woman he had ever met. And that was saying something considering when he was in the service, he had taken full advantage of Fleet Week in San Diego and

Hawaii, and really anytime he had gone ashore on leave.

His military uniform had been a damn magnet that he had reveled in.

But not a single one of the women he had met and spent the night fucking held a candle to Eve. It was in the grace of her movements, in the mixture of fragility and strength, in the sway of her hips, and the way she melted against him.

He jerked his chin to the passenger side door. "Get in."

"We're driving?" Surprise flitted over her features as he opened the passenger door so she could climb in.

Not so unemotional anymore, was she? "To the trailhead, and then from there we will go by foot."

"Ah, I see."

He shut the door once she was in her seat, and rounded the hood of the truck.

On the drive up into the mountains, they were both quiet. She seemed lost in thought, staring out the window.

But he had to know. "Have you ever camped before?"

"No. I don't know anything about it. I did do some research online, though, when I made the decision to do this." She glanced over at him. The sunglasses shielded her eyes, leaving him in the dark as to the emotions in them.

"One key to surviving this weekend intact is to do everything I ask the way I ask, and when."

"Sir, yes, Sir." She gave him a cheeky salute, and startled a laugh out of him. The woman was going to be a damn handful. But he was more than ready to get his hands on her if that was the case.

After pulling into an empty spot at the trailhead, they disembarked from the truck cab. He stowed her smaller pack in the larger one, then helped her into the hiking pack, making sure it was buckled properly. It also gave him an opportunity to touch her and watch how she reacted. She wasn't immune to him. He spied the racing pulse in her neck. It was enough for now.

"Is there a reason you're bringing a firearm on the camping trip?" Eve asked, nodding at the gun in the holster secured to his belt.

"The predator presence in the area has increased quite a bit. It's for protection, only as a last resort. The last thing I or the ranch wants is for a guest to be mauled by a hungry cougar. You need to remember, we're visitors in their home. They will attack if provoked or starving."

She seemed to absorb that information, and then nodded. "Got it."

He shouldered his pack, stowing his truck keys in one of the front pockets. Settling his ballcap over his head, he jerked his chin toward the trail. "Let's head out. We've got roughly a two-mile hike before we make camp."

"Lead the way."

It was cold out today. Tonight wouldn't be any better. But they had the thermal sleeping bags attached to their packs that would see them through the worst of it. On the way to the camp site, he pointed out various vegetation, and areas on the trail with loose gravel to avoid.

They came across deer tracks and he showed them to her. Eve was like a sponge, soaking up everything he told her. It was like she was filing the information away to use later.

It took the three of them an hour to reach the destination he had in mind for their campsite. It was a small clearing surrounded by pines and oak trees which helped shelter against the elements. Plus, there was already an area designated as the firepit, surrounded by rocks, in which they would light the campfire.

"First order of business is getting the tents set up. I want you to watch me as I set mine up. I will walk you through what I'm doing. And then, I will have you set yours up."

"Okay," she replied, laying her pack on the ground.

The tents were simple, four-man tents, which basically meant they were large enough to sleep four people in a sardine formation without much more room than that. "These are standard A-frames. When you're camping and need to bring everything with you, smaller is better. Unlike those glam tents with all the set up and flash extras."

"Are they anything like the tents you used in the military?"

He snorted. "Out on mission, we didn't sleep in tents. We slept on the ground. For me, sleeping in a tent is a major step up."

"But what if it rained or snowed or—"

He shot her a look. "That's the military, honey. Erecting a tent when you're in enemy territory is like waving a red cape at a bull, and puts a target on your back."

"Were you in enemy territory a lot?"

He studied her for a moment before responding. "More times than I can remember, and I never kept a tally. On mission, there are two goals: a successful mission, and living to see the next one. That's it."

"It couldn't have been easy."

It hadn't been. How many times had he boarded a chopper only to wonder if it would be for the last time? "No. It wasn't. But you're getting us off topic. When you're camping off grid, you want the easiest and sturdiest type of tent you can find. These A-frames are durable, waterproof, and easy to assemble and take down, while still being lightweight. Always remember when you camp to make your pack as light as possible while still having all the things you need."

She nodded as he took her through the steps one by one. For a minute, he was surprised she didn't have a notebook in her hands, taking notes as he erected his tent.

When he'd finished the demonstration, he glanced her way. "Now it's your turn."

Eve fumbled a bit as she unrolled the tent.

"Here, like this."

She shot him a glare. "I've got it. Thanks though. I need to learn this. I won't if you do it for me."

He crouched beside her as she assembled the stakes and poles. She was assembling it slower, but she had the gist of it. Then again, she was extremely smart. Likely smarter than him.

"Why do you want to learn this stuff?" His curiosity got the better of him. He wanted an explanation.

"They're good life skills, right?"

"So you're not planning on camping by yourself?" Just what was she trying to hide?

"I didn't say that, but I've never lived anywhere this remote before. After that snowstorm, I got thinking about all the things I don't know when it comes to survival. I mean, I couldn't even get the flue on the chimney open by myself." She shook her head as she inserted the poles, lifting the tent up.

"That wasn't your fault, honey. Lincoln told me the darn thing was rusted and faulty. There wasn't anything you could have done without getting it fixed."

"Yeah, well, next time I might not have a big strong man to protect me and fix it for me." She snorted derisively.

"Nothing wrong with a little self-reliance." But why did he get the feeling it was more than that? She was hiding something. He couldn't quite put his finger on it.

He didn't know if she was running from an ex who had beat her or what, although it seemed the most likely scenario—considering her hesitancy to take their tonsil hockey session to the next level.

"But that still doesn't tell me why you want to learn this stuff. What aren't you telling me?"

"I just don't want to be caught unawares ever again. And yeah, I have other reasons, but they are mine."

"Fair enough." He didn't say that he would get them out of her eventually. She was too interesting a puzzle for him not to solve.

When she had the tent erected, he checked it over, making sure it was sturdy for the nights head. "Good job.

Next up, we need to collect firewood so we can get a fire going a bit later."

"If we're not starting a fire right away, why are we getting the firewood now?"

"Because we want to make sure we collect enough before sunset. Once the temperature and wind chill drops, you're going to want to sit as close as you can to that fire, not be out in the dark, hunting up fuel. Remember, one of the keys to surviving in the wild is being smart and having the ability to anticipate what you will need."

"Good to know. So, where do we find firewood?"

"I'll show you. Come on." He rose, dusting his jeans off, and watched her do the same. She listened and followed his directions better than some of the enlisted soldiers he'd had under his command.

It made her this perfect, enticing woman and he craved to discover how she would respond to bedroom commands. Would she toss her braid over her shoulder and give him a taste of droll wit as she defied his orders, or would she melt into the perfect, obedient submissive, eager and willing to please?

Fuck, he wanted to find out.

And it was going to kill him to keep his hands off her for the next forty-eight hours.

11

*S*he shivered as the gust of cold wind blew around them. This was the first time camping for her, ever. Given the time of year, it was unbelievably cold. Even wearing multiple layers, the big thick coat she had purchased, a wool hat and snow gloves, wool socks and thermals underneath, she was still cold. It made her question her decision to go on this camping trip.

If it hadn't been for the instance at the hotel this week, she might not have jumped on the idea of taking this trip. Not when it was costing her almost her full paycheck, and that was with the employee discount. It was stupid, really. A case of mistaken identity, nothing more. She had seen a man in the hall on the second floor with his back to her, speaking on his cell phone. From behind, his height and bald head had given her a bad moment. She had almost peed in her pants, thinking that Trevor had found her.

She had spent the night after that incident tossing and turning over what she should do if he found her like that. Where would she go that was safe? It had gotten her thinking that perhaps she could disappear entirely in the wilderness. The only problem being she had no idea how to survive out in the wild.

But Duncan did. And while he had mentioned the other guides, she didn't know them. She would feel uncomfortable with other men alone on a camping trip.

At least the constant movement since they began establishing their campsite helped keep her warmer than if all they were doing was sitting before the fire. Because then, she'd be a frozen popsicle. Shivering, she wondered if she would find herself crawling into Duncan's tent in the middle of the night, not for any hanky panky, but for warmth.

Although, she wouldn't mind the hanky panky. In fact, she had decided that she was going to sleep with him. Because the incident this week had reminded her just how fragile life could be. The truth was that she had death stalking her like a demented girl scout trying to meet her cookie quota maniacally ringing her doorbell.

For some unexplainable reason, Duncan churned Eve up inside in ways few men ever had, and she didn't want to miss this chance.

Setting what hopefully would be the last load of firewood down, Duncan said, "That should get us through the night. We'll have to scout further afield tomorrow morning to replenish our supply."

Only until morning? "Is it going to get that cold?"

He leveled her with a glance. "It will. But the sleeping bags are thermal. Once you are inside them, they get quite toasty, and the tent buffers the wind. If the temperature drops too much, we'll share a tent, or I can have Sampson sleep in with you. I won't let you freeze, promise."

"Okay, what's next?" The thought of sharing a tent with Duncan made her toes curl.

"It's time to catch our dinner."

"What are we catching, and how?"

He grabbed a few items out of his backpack. "Follow me."

They walked through the woods with Sampson loping at their side. The dog was a sweetie pie, sticking with Eve while she gathered branches for their campfire. Duncan had likely told him to guard her. The pleasure she felt over it was absurd. But it had been ages since anyone had worried about her welfare.

Not since her parents had died seven years ago.

It was blissfully nice realizing that, while they didn't always agree, Duncan would stand watch over her, do what was necessary to make sure she was safe. She wanted to cling to him. Burrow into the protection he offered, and stay there.

He made her feel safe.

Even when he was a danger to her peace of mind and libido.

"We—and by we, I mean you—are going to catch us a fish for dinner tonight," Duncan said.

"We're having fish? And what makes you so sure they will bite?"

"They will, once I teach you my ways. Fishing is about patience. And yeah, we're a little late in the day, it's better to fish in the early morning typically, but we'll dine on fish tonight."

"I wish I had your confidence," she blurted before she realized she'd said it out loud. Sputtering, feeling her cheeks heat with embarrassment, she went on, "What I meant was—"

"Confidence is about trusting yourself. So, if you feel that's lacking, ask yourself why you don't trust yourself."

"I've made a lot of bad choices."

"Did you hurt other people with those choices?"

She tried to think of anyone but herself who had been impacted by those choices. "No. Myself mostly."

"Then perhaps you need to examine what other choice you might have had in those situations. Sometimes, there's only one way out of circumstances. What that means is that even though the consequences might not have been in your favor, it doesn't mean you can't trust yourself. Shit happens. It happens whether you're a good person or not; it's how you react when the chips are down and there's no chance of winning that defines you. If you stood your ground even when you knew you were going to lose, that is the very definition of courage. And that is something to feel confident about and trust in yourself. It takes far more bravery to get back up after being knocked down, than in never knowing defeat."

She swallowed the lump in her throat and nodded. None of the things Silas and Trevor had done were her fault—other than a bit of gullibility on her part. But she had been raised in a sheltered environment, and had never been exposed to con men or criminals. Changing the subject because she felt like weeping over Duncan's faith in her, she asked, "So how are we going to catch a fish? With our bare hands?"

"I recommend carrying one of these hooks in your camping pack anytime you go into the wilderness, in case you ever get stuck or stranded, because it means you won't starve. This and a bit of fishing line will ensure that you eat."

She stared at the silver metal with the curved point. "Can I buy one of those hooks in town?"

"Yep. The outdoor surplus should have them. I can pick one up for you next time I'm there," he offered, like it was the simplest thing in the world.

See, he was a good man. Silas certainly never offered to pick anything up for her, at least not without expecting something in return. And it was ridiculous that she was still using Silas as a measuring stick when it came to men.

"That would be nice. Thank you." She hated how much she liked that he seemed bent on going out of his way to take care of her.

"And we're going to attach them to this." He whipped out two silver rods no longer than the size of a pen.

"How's that?"

"I'll show you," Duncan commented with a wry grin.

The small rod expanded, he attached another piece to it then added the fishing line and hook. "You're like MacGyver with that thing."

He chuckled. "Now, it's your turn."

It took her much longer to assemble the compact fishing rod than it took him. But then, she had never done this type of thing. Once the rods were fully assembled, he taught her how to cast the hook into the water. And then they waited for a fish to bite.

They sat together in relative silence, each of them lost in thought. But it was a comfortable silence. She enjoyed his presence beside her on the rock they'd chosen to sit on to catch their dinner. It was cold, to be sure, but for the first time in forever, she didn't feel alone, even with the silence between them.

That had been one of the reasons she had fallen for Silas's lies. She had been achingly lonely, adrift, and still wrestling with her parents' deaths, staggering under the weight of responsibilities running the small-town bank her great-grandfather had started after the Great Depression.

There was a tug on her line that broke her from her reverie. She jolted when it tugged again. She gasped. "Duncan, I think I've got something. What do I do?"

His hand closed over hers. "Slowly, begin to turn the crank and reel him in."

Focusing on the task and not the fact that he was touching her, she turned the handle again and again.

"That's it. Steady," he murmured by her ear.

She shivered but kept up the pace on the fishing line, turning and pulling the fish closer. It struggled against her grip. For a second, she almost lost it. But then she tightened her hold on the pole. Using all her strength, she lifted the wriggling, gasping fish up out of the water.

And, like magic, Duncan produced a small net, scooping it underneath the squirming future meal.

He drew the net over land. "That's a good-sized trout... hell. Hold this for me."

He shoved the net into her hands. Eve felt bad for the little guy. But then she watched Duncan, who wasted no movements as he reeled in his line. The concentration on his face sent tingles racing along her spine. He'd had the same kind of focus the other night... when they were kissing.

He lifted the line, pulling a second trout from the stream. "We're eating like kings tonight."

He shifted and brought the pole over land, a broad smile on his face, then explained the proper way to get them off the fish hook.

"Now, the next part is a little messy. I'll show you how to debone and remove the guts from our catch."

Her stomach roiled. "Okay. I want to apologize in advance if it makes me puke."

Duncan took her through the steps. Placing the fish on a flat rock, he took a knife he produced from another pocket, and cut along the belly. She fought her gorge as he demonstrated how to remove the guts and then the bones.

She gagged, and decided for the next little bit, she wasn't breathing through her nose.

"All right, your turn." He handed her the knife.

She stared at the helpless fish still gasping its final few breaths. "I'm sorry," she said to the fish.

Taking the knife, she cut in a straight line along its belly.

"Good, now removed the intestines like I showed you."

Before she lost her nerve, she shoved her fingers

inside the fish, which was still warm. She found the sack and pulled, fighting her gorge the entire time.

"Good. Now the bone. And really give it a good yank," he instructed.

Trying not to process what she was doing, she removed the bone with a firm tug.

"Ha ha! Well done, Eve. Here, give it to me. Go wash your hands in the stream," he ordered.

Eve headed back to the stream. Her hands shook as she washed them in the icy mountain water, scrubbing them to remove the blood and guts. She'd done it. Even though it made her sick to her stomach. She had accomplished a major feat. While she wasn't nearly ready to go it alone yet, she bet that with practice, she would get better.

Duncan showed her how to dispose of the fish guts and bones without making her do it. "Sampson, nuh-uh, bud. I don't think so."

"What was he doing?" She studied the dog who sat with his head bent, looking at Duncan with sad eyes.

"Sampson has a bad habit. On our camping trips, he likes to roll in fish guts and bear shit. Don't ask me why, since he's a bit of a knucklehead. But he always looks like he's having a great time while he does it. Only then he ends up reeking for the remainder of the trip."

"Got it. Keep him away from both."

"Let's get these back to camp, and we'll get the fire going. Then we will toss these bad boys over the flames and get dinner started."

"I'm not hungry." Not after the whole removing of the guts and bone.

"You will be, and that's the point. While it's not fun to do, the result is a hearty, protein-packed meal."

They would see about that. They headed back to the campsite. Duncan showed her the firestarter that he carried in his backpack, and showed her the best way to arrange the wood. Then he got the fire going. From his pack, he produced a small expandable fire grate and laid the cleaned fish directly on the grate.

From his pack, he produced a small pot, dumped a bag of something into it with some water, and laid it over the grate too.

"It smells good."

"It will taste even better."

"Oh, I brought some snacks too. I've got cookies."

"The chocolate chip ones?" he asked.

"Yep."

"See? We're feasting like royalty tonight. We need to set up the bear bag. Bring all the treats out, and we'll get the bag stored. This way, we won't have any curious visitors overnight, hoping to get to our food supplies."

She went and grabbed the smaller bag from inside the pack that held all the treats. Duncan had a sturdy looking black bag sitting on the ground with a length of rope. "Put whatever we don't need for tonight in that. Then we're going to hang it up on a tree."

"Got it." She removed a few cookies before putting the rest inside, on top of what he had already stowed in there.

"Let's go hang this up real quick. Sampson, come on. Now, we're going to use a tree about two hundred feet from our campsite. There is one that I like to use when I bring campers here. And we want to hang it fifteen to twenty feet off the ground. That should keep it from any curious bears or critters."

Duncan showed her how to get the rope over a sturdy limb, attach the bag to the rope, and then secure the bag up off the ground.

On the way back to camp, with dark settling around them, she asked, "You have to store food that way every time you camp?"

"Yep. And the bag and rope are the easiest method, especially for backpack camping, which is what we're doing."

By the time dinner had finished cooking, the sun had set, and temperatures plummeted even further. Duncan produced two mess kit plates with utensils. They sat around the fire, dining on trout and rice with mixed vegetables.

And he had been right. The smell of the sizzling fish had made her mouth water. When they were done, she broke out the cookies she had held back from the bear bag.

"What else did you bring in that bag?"

"Some cinnamon chip scones, and apples for breakfast."

He groaned around a bite of a chocolate chip cookie. "I've got eggs and coffee. Breakfast will be stellar. I should take you camping with me more often if this is how I get to eat."

She blushed at the compliment and was thankful for the dark, hoping it hid most of it. "Thank you."

"For what? You did a lot of the work."

"For not telling me I was crazy to want to learn this stuff, and canceling the camping trip."

"Why do you feel you need to be self-reliant like this? Not that it's a bad thing, because it's not, but it does make me curious."

The man was like a dog with a bone. He'd asked her a similar question earlier. She was quiet for a moment, trying to decide how much to tell him. Because he was the first person in a very long time she wanted to confide in. But she still had to be careful. Duncan was an honorable man, who always did the right thing. In the last year, she had committed fraud by changing her name and identity every time she had been forced to move. She had lied about almost everything. And yet, for some reason, she didn't want to lie to him.

"It's okay if—"

She cut him off. "I trusted someone I shouldn't have, and I'm still experiencing the fallout because of it. It was my mistake to trust him."

"Did he hurt you?"

At the question, the night that Trevor attacked her in her home played like a bad movie in her brain. Images from the past year ran through her mind. The sleepless nights in rundown motels, the diners with the sketchy bosses that didn't mind copping a feel and pretended ignorance when you asked them not to, the fear of looking over her shoulder, waiting for the hammer blow to finish off the last pathetic thread of her life. Had Trevor hurt her? He had done nothing but that. "Yes. I fought back, and got away."

"And you still don't trust yourself?"

"He had reasons—"

"Bullshit! There's no reason for attacking a woman. Unless you were coming at him with a machete, there's no excuse." His face had hardened. His gaze glinted like sharp blades in the firelight. "There was no one there to help you?"

She shook her head. "No."

Not even the police had helped. All they had done was put a warrant out on him and contacted the parole board. Told her to get an alarm system, and file a request for an order of protection. A lot of good a piece of paper would do her when Trevor was attempting to strangle her to death—or worse.

"I'm sorry. It's not easy being on your own."

"You sound like you know what it's like."

"I do. But I consider the people on this ranch my family just as much as I considered my SEAL brothers my family. We look out for one another, help one another out when needed."

"It sounds nice."

"If you're here long enough, you'll be welcomed into the fold too. We've got good people at the ranch."

"I'm coming to see that." Eve hoped that she would be there long enough to experience that camaraderie. While she wasn't a huge fan of the job, the people, her cabin, and the pay weren't bad. If she was there long enough, maybe she could move to an administrative role in one of the offices.

She yawned, staring into the hypnotic dance of the flames.

"Why don't you get some sleep? We've got a long day of instruction tomorrow, and start at first light."

"I just need to..." She blushed. Nothing like needing to tell a man you need to find a bush so you can pee.

"Don't go too far. Holler if you need anything."

"Okay." Her face flaming, she felt his gaze follow her into the trees.

She wasn't prepared for how dark it was even as she marveled at the beauty of the Milky Way. After a quick trip to relieve herself in the bushes, she returned to camp.

"Goodnight," she murmured.

"Night, Eve." Duncan stayed before the fire, like he was keeping watch.

But the day had caught up with her. Something about the mountain air, the cold, and the physical activity had taken its toll. She crawled into her tent, zipping the flap shut to help keep the wind out. Removing her hiking boots and coat, she climbed into the sleeping bag, zipping herself in. Her shivering stopped as the thermal warmth of the sleeping bag surrounded her.

Duncan was right, damn him. Snuggling further into the sleeping bag, convinced she was going to have a hell of time sleeping on the ground, she closed her eyes. Surprisingly, she dropped off like a stone tossed into a lake.

Visions of the past beset her dreams, turning what should have been a pleasant night into a horror show. How many times would he get to her?

In the dream, Trevor was chasing her down a long hall, shouting that he was going to get her and gut her like a fish. As she ran, she checked all the doors, looking for an escape hatch, but none of the doors would open. He just kept coming. There was no way out. She whimpered as she ran, her legs straining. They ached from running.

The next thing she knew, something touched her shoulder and gave it a little shake. Her eyes snapped open. She struggled against the hand with a frightened scream.

"Hey, it's just me. You were crying in your sleep and disturbing Sampson." Duncan's calm voice doused the rising panic, along with the beam of light from his flashlight.

She hated the constant fear and worry, and squeezed her eyes shut to quell the onslaught of tears. "Sorry. Bad dreams. I didn't mean to wake you."

"I get them too. I get it. Just remember, nothing is going to harm you while I'm around, okay?" he said, and moved back toward the tent door.

"Duncan," she whispered, needing his steady presence like a lifeline.

"Yeah?" he grunted.

"Would you stay in here? I don't want to be alone. I —" She bit her bottom lip to contain the sob.

"Let me grab my bag. I'll be right back." Duncan didn't chastise her, or tell her she was being overly dramatic.

He left the tent. The wind whistled through the open flaps, making her shiver. He was gone for a hot minute— long enough, she started to wonder if he was coming back. She listened for his footsteps and didn't hear a thing.

But then he and Sampson entered the tent. Sampson

sniffed her face. His hot doggy breath washed over her face. Not saying a word after he zipped the tent back up, sealing them inside, Duncan unrolled his sleeping bag. The light from his flashlight cast his face in shadows. He hadn't hesitated to come to her aid. Through lowered lashes, she watched as he removed his boots. The intimacy of the gesture wasn't lost on her.

They settled in beside her, with Sampson snuggling down between them. With the big dog's body pressed against her side, Eve felt the tension in her system relax by degrees. She didn't have to face the dark and night alone.

It meant the world to her in ways she couldn't explain to him. But it mattered.

After he shut the flashlight off, she murmured, "Thank you."

"Anytime, Eve. Get some sleep. Morning will be here before you know it."

His solid presence in the tent lulled her back to sleep. And boy did she sleep, sounder and deeper than she had in months.

She slept so deeply that when he nudged her awake with soft words and a gentle touch, she lifted bleary eyes. Gone was his ballcap. Scruffy stubble lined his jaw, his short hair was in disarray, and yet he was more handsome than any of the men in three-piece suits who had visited the bank.

It took everything inside her not to reach for him, when the thought of being in his arms made it impossible to resist his magnetic lure. Much like the fish last night, she wanted him to catch her.

"Sorry to wake you when you look so peaceful, but we need to get a move on if we're going to fit everything in today."

She nodded. "Give me a minute and I will be right out."

"See you outside." He exited the tent. Sampson was already gone.

Eve pressed her hand against her chest to stop the sudden ache. Boy, did she have it bad where Duncan was concerned. She didn't understand her fascination. All she could do was pray that she didn't get burned.

*a*fter donning a clean shirt, panties, and fresh pair of socks, Eve used one of the facial cleansing cloths she had packed in her bag. She might be in the great outdoors, but that didn't mean she wasn't going to clean her face, put on deodorant, or brush her teeth after they ate some breakfast.

Dressed and ready for the day ahead, she exited the tent. Sampson was nose deep in a bowl of dog chow.

While she had dressed, Duncan had grabbed the bear bag with their food. Eve and Duncan worked in concert to put breakfast together. He had her start the fire with a fresh pile of firewood. She followed the steps he had instructed her to use the day before. As the flames sparked, licking over the wood, she smiled at the small victory.

She divvied up one of the apples between the two mess kit plates while he made eggs and coffee. They were the powdered kind of egg but would do for today. Then she withdrew the bag of scones from the bear bag. She put two of the cinnamon chip scones on his plate, and one for herself. There was enough if they wanted a snack this afternoon, and also enough for breakfast tomorrow morning.

Sampson was at her side, sniffing what she had in her hands.

"You think I've got something for you too?" she teased the pup, who just looked at her with big, brown, soulful eyes full of hope.

"Sampson, don't beg."

"Oh, he's fine. Besides, he's right, I do have something for him."

Sampson's tail started wagging fast, like he knew she meant him. His ears perked up and if asked, she'd have said his expression was downright happily eager.

"You do?" Duncan asked with surprise clouding his voice.

"Yep. When I decided to do this trip, I figured that if I was going to make treats for us to eat, I should make some for Sampson too." She put the plates on a nearby flat rock so Duncan could divvy up the eggs. Storing the rest of the scones back in the bear bag, she pulled out another sack.

"And these are for you. Just one for right now, but if you like them, I have more back at the cabin too." She withdrew one of the peanut butter flavored dog treats she had baked on a whim the other night.

"You made dog bone treats from scratch?"

She nodded, her focus on Sampson. "Yes, I did. Sit, Sampson."

The German Shephard plopped his butt down at the

command, his nose sniffing the air. She held the treat out for him. He nipped it cleanly from her fingers, much to her delight, laughing as he scarfed it down in a few large bites before shooting her another hopeful grin. She'd not had a dog since she had been a teenager. As an adult, she'd just never had the time.

She scratched him behind the ears. "You seem to like them. You can have more later, okay?"

Sampson harrumphed as she stored the rest of them back in the bag. Duncan handed her the mess kit plate with her breakfast. "You've done it now."

"What do you mean?"

Fighting back a smile and losing, he jerked his chin toward his dog, who currently sat by her side with his head in her lap. "Once you feed him, even something as simple as a treat, he's your best bud. And he likes to charm all the ladies."

"Do you get a lot of women doing these camping trips?" She was curious if she was an oddity or not in wanting to learn outdoor survival skills.

"Here and there. Most often, I get fathers and sons."

"So, you've never had an all-female trip?"

"I didn't say that." Duncan took a bite of a scone and groaned heartily. "Holy shit, these are good. What else do you bake, or is it just cookies and scones? And where did you learn to bake like this?"

"I love all things baking: cookies, muffins, cakes, pies, scones, pastries, bread, brownies. It's kind of an obsession, to be honest. It soothes me when I'm stressed. I took a lot of cooking classes, went to culinary school for baking.

The timing was off with culinary school and I only completed a semester, but I've always loved baking."

"You should open a bakery. People would pay loads to eat your stuff."

Pleasure suffused her at the compliment. "Appreciate it. I've considered that."

"Is it just baking, or cooking too? Because if memory serves, you can do that as well."

"I like cooking. I'm good at it. But I've always thought that I excel at baking." She nibbled on her scone, more focused on watching him eat. She' never knew watching a person eat when they were fully enjoying their meal could be sexy as hell.

Duncan polished off both his scones before she had finished one. He glanced at her half-eaten plate then lifted his gaze to her face. "Not to rush you, but if we're going to fit everything in before nightfall, we need to get a move on in the next ten minutes."

There were only a few bites left of her scone, and she was full. She held it out to Sampson, who happily scarfed down the treat and stared at her adoringly. She gave him a kiss on the head, enjoying the big, goofy pup's presence. If she stayed in Colorado, it was something she would do for herself—adopt a dog. A big one like Sampson, who could be both a companion and a protector in a tight spot.

They washed the plates off in the nearby stream before Duncan showed her how to store the food for the day. He had her haul the bear bag up into the tree and secure the rope properly.

"All right, we've got that task out of the way. With the

fire still going in the firepit, we're going to collect water, boil, and store it for use."

"Is that something you always have to do, boil water?" she asked as he pulled something out of his backpack.

"Yes. Unless you bring bottled water with you, which is difficult to bring enough when you are backpacking it. Boiling water is the easiest way of getting rid of parasites and bacteria that can make you sick. Let's take the pot down to the stream. We're going to fill it with water and boil it for at least five minutes. We'll let it cool, and then store it in this collapsible jug."

She followed him down to the stream. They filled the pot with water. She carried it back, still curious. "So is boiling the only way to remove contaminants from water?"

"You can also use either chlorine or iodine tablets. They're fairly portable. And you just drop a pill into a bottle of water. You need to give it about sixty minutes for it to be effective. There are also water filters you can get. I'll show you one. Why don't you set the pan to boil over the flames?" He nodded toward the fire.

He withdrew a compact pouch about eight inches long, opened it up, and withdrew a small blue device. "This is a Lifestraw. They're cheap, easy to carry, and effective. You can put this straw directly into the stream and drink. It filters out all the harmful stuff. They have larger filters to add to a bag with a filter on one end that you then squeeze into a bottle."

"That's really pretty cool. I didn't know any of that." It was extremely useful information.

Once they had finished boiling water, they stored it in the collapsible jug.

When that task was complete, they took a small hike. "The purpose of this exercise is to identify edible plants, at least those here in Colorado. They can differ by region, so before you go somewhere, make sure you look up what's there. If you're stuck out in the wilderness without food, say you lost your trusty fish hook and need to eat, knowing which plants in the area are edible can go a long way to protecting you from starvation."

She followed him through the dense trees as they walked along the stream. He pointed out wild asparagus, morels, wild strawberries, wild plums, dandelions, orache, and porcini mushrooms. She took notes in a small spiral notebook she had packed, much to Duncan's amusement.

"The porcini look similar to mushrooms that are not edible, and are actually poisonous. So, good rule of thumb is, if you aren't sure what it is or aren't a hundred percent sure that you have identified it correctly, don't eat it. Because it could mean the difference between life and death."

"Got it. I might need to get a book on edible plants after this so I can start to identify them better."

"It's not a half bad idea. Especially if you plan on camping a lot. The more you do it, the more you will start to recognize them on sight. Come on. Let's head back to camp. I want to show you how to build shelter when you don't have a tent handy."

"Lead the way." She gestured.

The day passed by in a blur as he went through a few

different ways of building emergency shelter with a tarp. He had her try the different methods before they broke for a quick lunch of apples and protein bars.

In the afternoon, they gathered more firewood for the night ahead before heading off on a second hike, this time in the opposite direction. This time, it was about identifying various animal tracks. On their trek, they came across a herd of mule deer. Eve stood still at Duncan's side, watching as the small herd meandered on their way. They were majestic and beautiful. Even Sampson sat at their side and didn't approach the deer—likely because Duncan ordered him to stay.

They headed back to camp shortly after seeing the deer. Once there, Duncan handed her the fishing pole and hook. He had her do the fishing that afternoon to catch dinner. He was with her the whole time, but he wanted her to learn it, and was hands off, only stepping in if she had a question, which she appreciated. By doing it herself, she was learning it and committing it to memory. And that was the point of the exercise.

She caught two fish, then had to remove the guts and debone them herself. At least Duncan did help her with the clean-up.

Back at camp, though, he had her build the fire and get the fish cooking. With the bear bag down, he pulled out a dried food pack of rice and veggies again, and showed her how to get that going over the makeshift campfire stove. He took out more of the cookies and some biscuits for Sampson before storing it back up off the ground.

By the time they sat down to dinner to actually eat,

on a flat log that Duncan had found earlier in the day for them to sit on instead of the ground, Eve was ravenous, and plowed through the meal with gusto. She almost licked the plate clean, the food was so good. And even with the hard work of maintaining the campsite, she was having fun. It was in large part due to the man with her. She was glad she'd chosen him.

After cleaning up the pan and plates, she needed to make a trip to the bushes. She did miss indoor plumbing. "I'll be back in a minute."

"Don't go too far. Yell if you need me."

The deep resonance of his baritone followed her into the bushes as darkness surrounded her. It was time to take what she wanted for a change. Stop living on the sidelines, grab life by the proverbial horn, and ride that bull.

Or a cowboy.

Tonight, when she went to bed, she wouldn't be doing it alone.

13

On her way back to the firepit and Duncan, Eve stopped at her tent. She withdrew the small bottle of whiskey that she had been saving. Now that they had spent a solid twenty-four hours together, she figured a little lubricant would help get them started, and ease her lingering anxiety.

The thing was, all day long, she had caught him looking at her. And not just glancing over to make sure she didn't need any help, but really looking, with admiration and lust blazing in those dark depths of his eyes.

She wanted Duncan, more than she had ever wanted another man before. The time was right. It felt right to give in to the need she couldn't seem to escape anytime he was near.

With a deep, calming breath, she left the tent and headed to her seat beside him on the log. She sat, and showed him the bottle in her hands. "I figured it was a good time to break this out."

He chuckled, with a lopsided grin on his face. "You are chock full of surprises. No girly drinks for you."

"Oh, I like cocktails, the girlier the better, but that doesn't mean I can't appreciate a good whiskey or scotch. I've tried this one before. It's from a distillery in Colorado, Meath Irish Distillery." She uncapped the bottle, took a swig, and handed it to him.

The amber liquid burned smoothly as it traveled into her belly. The liquor warmed her from the inside out, while the fire and Duncan's closeness warmed the outside.

"What was it like, being a SEAL?" She took the bottle back and stared at him over the rim before she drank another long dram of the alcohol.

Duncan studied her. The firelight cast a golden glow on his features as night darkened.

"If you don't want to—"

"It's not that. I just normally don't talk about my time in the Navy. Not that I'm ashamed by it... it's more that everything I did, that I experienced, can be difficult to understand if you've not been in it."

"Try." She passed him back the bottle.

He took a long drink, pegged her with an intense stare, and said, "I entered the Navy directly out of high school. My dad was a Naval officer. I knew by the time I was thirteen that I would be following him into the service. But I didn't want to be an officer. I wanted to be in the thick of the fighting, which is why I decided to try for the SEALs. It's brutal training, pushes you so far past your comfort limits, it eradicates them completely. It's taxing physically, mentally, and emotionally."

"You sound like you loved it." Taking the proffered bottle, she took another swig before handing it back.

"I did. I've always been a bit of an adrenaline junkie. Being a SEAL fulfilled that side of me better than anything else I had tried. It's dangerous work. I can't tell you how many tight spots my unit and I found ourselves in."

"Too many to remember?"

He shook his head. "No. Too many that are classified. It was bloody and brutal, living one day and one mission at a time. Plenty of time spent behind enemy lines, doing things that I can't take back."

"You shot people." It was a statement, not a question really. He couldn't have been on missions like that and not have shot at people.

Duncan pegged her with a frank stare. "I didn't just shoot people, I killed them. I didn't have a desk job where I never saw any action. I was in the thick of it daily for twelve years."

She digested that bit of information. It had to be hard for him, knowing he had taken lives and living with that, accepting it every day. She marveled at the strength of his character. "And why did you leave?"

His brows rose at her question, like he had expected her to blast him, cast him into the role of villain.

But that was something she couldn't do. And while they hadn't had the most auspicious start, they had moved past all that.

"On a mission in Kandahar, I was shot."

"You what? Where?" Her gaze slid over him, looking for any sign of the injury.

"Right below my left knee. Broke my leg in the process. Once they removed the bullet, they had to insert some rods. I was flown from Afghanistan to a base in Germany and then finally, once I was stable enough, back to Walter Reed in DC for the rest of my recovery. With my injury, there was no way I could serve any longer. Just a jump out of a plane could cause my leg to buckle. So I was honorably discharged, and awarded some medals on my way out the door. I had already been planning on retiring in a year or so, the injury just made that retirement happen sooner."

"I'm sorry. That couldn't have been easy."

He handed her the bottle. But she shook her head. If she had any more, she would be tossing the cookies up in the bushes, instead of making a move. And she yearned to get her hands on him more than she wanted another sip.

"It wasn't, at the time. But looking back, if the bullet had hit much higher, my story would have ended right then. I would have bled out on the street. It worked out in the end. I've got a great life here, one I wouldn't trade for anything."

"Yeah, teaching people who don't have a clue what they are doing out in the wild how to survive."

He shrugged at her teasing. "It's work I enjoy. We should get some sleep. It will be light before you know it."

Eve glanced at him. At the bottle of whiskey on the ground between them, leaning against the log. He was handsome, in a rugged, uber-masculine way. In all her life, she had never wanted a man the way she wanted him. She knew too well what having the life you'd led ripped from you unexpectedly could do to your psyche and sense of self. He awed her. He could have allowed the loss to make him bitter, but instead he had adapted.

With the warmth of the whiskey filling her with confidence she didn't normally feel in these situations, she leaned in. Before she could tell herself to stop, she cupped his face between her hands, his scruff scraping her palms, and planted her mouth over his lips.

Eve kissed him while he sat stock still, not reaching for her or doing anything. She could taste the whiskey on his lips as she ran her tongue along the seam, seeking entry.

Duncan gripped her biceps. With an expletive, he ripped his mouth away. The storm of the century entered his gaze as he snarled, "What the hell do you think you're doing?'

Undeterred, she replied drolly, "I figured it was obvious."

"I told you not to kiss me unless you planned to see it through. I won't do this yo-yo bullshit where you put the brakes on." He shot to his feet, yanked her up, then steered her to her tent, as if she was a recalcitrant child being taken to her room.

"What are you going to do, spank me?"

"I should," he growled through clenched teeth. He opened the entrance to her tent and jerked his head toward the entrance. He chewed out, "Go. To. Bed."

"I will. But not alone." She ran her hands over his chest. There was no give in his muscles—not that she expected any. The soft flannel material covering his firm chest needed to go. She wanted to feel his warm skin beneath, taste him. Run her nails through his chest hair and capture the lightning bolt of his strength.

Rather emboldened when he didn't move away from her touch, she stepped into him until there was a hair's breadth of space. Taking it one step further, she kept her gaze on his. Shadows flickered, keeping part of his face hidden. Not waiting for an invitation, she cupped him through his jeans. "I'm not running."

Jesus, he was big. Flames licked outward from her core, spreading until she buzzed with such potent need, she thought she might erupt into flames.

He gripped her shoulders, like he intended to thrust her away, chastise her for her actions, and erect barriers that would be insurmountable.

"Fuck." He muttered the soft curse.

His lips crashed over hers with stunning ferocity. One minute, she was cupping him through his jeans, and the next, she was holding on for dear life as her bones melted. He sealed his mouth firmly over hers, his tongue parting her lips as he invaded the furthest recesses of her mouth.

Duncan plundered as he tangled their tongues together, showing her that while she might have started it, he would finish it. She had waved herself in front of a snorting bull, and now she was the one ensnared in its horns.

Duncan lifted her up as if she weighed nothing, bent down, and entered her tent without breaking their connection. Her sex throbbed in eager anticipation. She wanted him. Here. Now. Hard. Fast.

He laid her on the sleeping bag, and finally lifted his

mouth. "Be sure. I kiss you again, I doubt I will be able to stop."

She placed her palm against his stubble-roughened cheek. "I want you, Duncan. Be with me."

On a guttural groan, he claimed her lips for a torrid exchange, settling himself between her thighs. She wrapped her legs around his waist, beyond aroused at this point. She loved the feel of his weight on top of her, the firmness of his chest pressed against hers.

The only problem was, they were wearing far too many clothes.

She shoved her hands beneath his coat, pushing the material aside. He helped her remove it when it became stuck on his muscular arms. He turned, and knelt. "Stay outside the tent, bud. We'll let you in when we're done."

Duncan zipped up the tent, keeping the wind out.

Eve took that opportunity to remove her boots and coat. When her hands went to her jeans, he stopped her. "Let me. I've fantasized about removing them—and what you have on underneath—with my teeth."

She bit her lip and nodded as need flash fried her system. *Holy moly!*

Duncan desired her every bit as much as she wanted him. He pushed her down and lay at her side. Leaning down, he kissed her in a drugging, curl-her-toes-until-she-was-his-willing-slave kind of way. As he kissed her brainless, his fingers worked at the buttons on her flannel shirt. He parted the material, his mouth never leaving hers as he helped her remove it from her body.

His hands slid beneath the long-sleeved thermal top. The rough pads of his fingers scraped over her skin as he lifted the shirt up her torso. He had to break the kiss for just a moment to lift her top over her head and off her arms.

But he didn't stop there; he lightly traced the edges of her lace bra. Her nipples beaded at his touch. With a flick of his hand, he undid the front clasp. Her breast spilled free.

On a deep groan, he murmured, "Fuck, you're beautiful."

Before she could thank him, he swooped down and sucked one of the buds into his hot mouth. She arched up off the sleeping bag, threaded her fingers through his hair, and held on tight.

He laved and nipped at the bud, suctioning her breast deep inside until she was writhing and gasping at the deluge of fire coursing through her. It had never been like this with anyone. He kneaded her other breast with his hand while he bit down on the engorged flesh.

She hissed. It hurt, but it was a good hurt. One that sent her system into overdrive at the megawatt volts erupting from her nipple shooting straight to her groin, making her sex pulsate in time with his tongue flicking against the bud. When her nipple was so swollen it ached, he switched to its twin, repeating the intense, thorough manipulation.

"Duncan, please," she begged him, already so far gone, she was ready to launch into the heavens.

He finally lifted his dark head. In the tent, she could barely make out his facial features. "Oh honey, we've barely begun." He drew a hand down over her torso to the waistband of her jeans. "This isn't going to be quick or easy. I'm going to make you come screaming my name so many times, you will be hoarse by morning."

"Oh god."

"Not even close. Surrender, Eve, give me everything, and I swear to you I will make it worth your while."

"Do your worst. I'm not going anywhere."

He chuckled darkly. Then, with his gaze on her face, he undid her jeans. The sound of her zipper lowering filled the tent, along with their panting breaths. His fingers teased the lace of her panties. "Are you wet for me, Eve?"

"Yes."

"Hmm, let's see, shall we?" He slid his hand beneath the lace. He delved between her folds.

She moaned as he rubbed her clit.

"Jesus, you're fucking drenched." He groaned as he withdrew his hand. Repositioning himself on his knees between her legs, he hooked his fingers around the waistband of her jeans and panties, drawing them down and off until she was completely bare.

"Take off your clothes."

"I'd better not. I don't have a condom with me, honey. But I can make you feel good tonight."

She smiled. She had planned for every scenario this weekend. "I do. Front pocket of my backpack. Now, take off your clothes."

"Bossy little thing."

She heard the zipper on her pack being opened.

"Rather sure of yourself, aren't you?" He put the string of foil packets on the ground beside the sleeping bag.

"No. But I want you and knew if there was a chance, I wanted to be prepared."

"You just earned an A in survival skills," he said, rising, stripping out of his jeans and boxers.

She caught glimpses in the shadows of rounded pecs, tight abs, powerful thighs, but it was his hard cock jutting from his apex that had her biting her lip. He was beautiful.

Then he knelt between her thighs, but he didn't kiss her. Not on the mouth, anyway. He parted her thighs wide to accommodate the sheer breadth of his shoulders. His fingers stroked from her clit all the way to her naughty back entrance. She shivered when he caressed that channel.

She had never considered anal sex until now, that she might be interested in trying it. But his touch there sent greedy flames licking over her skin that pooled in her pussy.

His mouth surrounded her clit and he sucked on the bud. Hard.

Pleasure lanced through her, arching her back, and she cried out at the intensity. But Duncan didn't stop or slow down. He swirled his tongue over and around her clit, with long drawn out laves and fast flicks that had her hips jerking at the waves of pleasure smashing into her.

When he plunged his tongue into her channel with a sexy groan that rattled in his chest, she almost came up off the ground. Her hips bucked. She threaded her fingers through his hair as he ate at her flesh.

"Duncan," she pleaded as she rocked.

He clamped his hands on her hips, not letting her

escape his coordinated assault on her sensitive flesh. She'd had men go down on her before, but none of them had known their way around a pussy like Duncan. He knew all the right places to touch and tease until she was a mindless, writhing mess, begging him for release.

"Please, Duncan, please."

He growled against her clit, vibrating the swollen nub.

Her jaw dropped open as he pressed a finger against her entrance and penetrated her sheath, sliding it all the way in. She whimpered as he began to thrust his finger while he sucked on her clit. He added a second finger and then a third, pumping them in and out.

She clung to him, digging her fingers into his shoulders, as if she were holding on for dear life. Moans spilled from her lips, echoing around the campsite. She was being loud enough, she was likely scaring away any predators. But she didn't care.

He bit down on her clit just as he plunged three fingers inside, and she imploded. Her toes curled, her back arched, and her hips bucked as she came.

"Duncan."

"That's it, honey. Take your pleasure," he commanded, thrusting his fingers as she clenched and rippled around him.

In a daze, she felt him move around. The sound of a foil packet ripping had her core tightening.

Then he stroked the head of his cock through her swollen pussy. Positioning the crest at her entrance, he eased inside. If she'd thought his fingers had felt amazing, his huge dick stretched her near the point of pain, and was downright incredible. He seated himself fully. Her pussy quivered around his shaft.

Duncan leaned down, propping himself up on his elbows so that their torsos were aligned. Her hands slid onto his back, the muscles rippling beneath her touch. Instinctively, she brought her legs up around his waist.

"Fuck me, but you're tight. I'm going to apologize if my performance is abbreviated tonight."

"It's been a while."

"Has it?"

"Yes."

"How long?"

"Not important. Now, are you going to fuck me, or are we going to talk all night?"

He barked out a laugh. "Oh, you're a bossy one all right. But here's a little something you need to know, honey. I'm a Dominant. And that's the kind of thing we like to dole out spankings for."

The thought of him spanking her made her pussy clench around his embedded cock. She huffed. "Promises, promises."

"I'm going to make you eat those words."

"Fine. You can spank me later." She clenched her Kegels, constricting his massive shaft.

He lowered his forehead to hers. "Are you trying to make me blow my wad?"

"No. Not yet. I just need—"

"Stop trying to control everything."

"But I just... oh, my god." She moaned as he withdrew and plunged so hard, it rattled her bones. "Again."

She didn't care that she was begging. She rocked and

wiggled her hips, clenching her pussy around his shaft again. Then she lost all sense of reason as her actions seemed to throw a switch in Duncan.

Propping himself up on his hands, he thrust hard and fast. His hips beat a smacking rhythm against hers as he power drilled her pussy with a ferocity that left her breathless and straining.

She canted her hips, rocking to meet his thunderous thrusts. Her hands slid down to his ass, and dug in. She moaned and writhed beneath him.

She'd asked him to fuck her, and that was precisely what he was doing. Her breathing grew choppy as she undulated. Sex with Duncan was better than anything she could have imagined. His grunts fueled the fire inside her to epic heights.

"Fuck, your pussy is insane," he groaned, plunging deep.

Eve went supernova as the climax slammed into her, his words setting her body off like a match tossed on top of a powder keg. Her pussy spasmed around his plowing shaft and seemed to have a ripple effect, sending him over the edge into uncontrollable bliss alongside her.

"Oh fuck, honey... ahhh." He strained, fucking her wildly as he came.

He disintegrated, collapsing on top of her with his head buried in the crook of her neck. He was still buried deep inside her, still a part of her, surrounding her body with his. She felt small and dainty beneath his much bigger form. She lightly traced his back with her fingertips, enjoying the firm press of his chest against hers.

"I'll move in a minute."

She pressed a kiss against his neck. "I like you right where you are."

She felt his lips shift into a grin against her neck. "Is that right?"

"Mmmhmm. Puts you in the right position for round two."

"Round two? You think there's going to be another round tonight?"

"Isn't there?" She opened her eyes to find his face hovering above hers, and clenched her Kegels around his shaft.

"Oh honey, you asked for it. Remember that," he murmured, and took her mouth for a sensual kiss.

She would remember it, all right—as one of the best nights of her life.

14

*P*leasure zipped along Duncan's spine and snapped his eyes open. He almost didn't believe what he was seeing and likely wouldn't have, if it didn't feel fucking amazing.

Eve's gaze connected with his as she bobbed up and down the length of his dick.

After their exploits overnight, he wouldn't have thought he would be ready again so soon. But there was something about Eve. When she had come on to him last night, a part of him had wondered if it had been the alcohol talking. Not that it had stopped him when she'd palmed him through his jeans because it hadn't. The moment she had touched him, he'd been a fucking goner.

And they had gorged on each other. At one point, he'd connected their sleeping bags together so they could stay warm as they reached for each other again and again throughout the night.

She was naked, her breasts swaying as she sucked his

shaft. He groaned, rocking his hips as she savored him in her mouth.

"Eve." He said her name like a benediction.

She lifted her mouth and cast him a seductive smile. "Morning. I was... hungry."

"Don't let me stop you." Waking up to a blow job with her hot little mouth sucking him off was the best way he'd woken up in ages—years, even.

She lifted a foil packet up. Ripped it open. Giving her her lead, he let her roll the condom down his length. He made no move to take her, wanting it to come from her. He gazed at her fucking knockout form as she straddled him.

Her breasts were high and firm, and filled his palms nicely with rouge-tipped thick nipples that jutted out, begging for a pair of lips to suck them. Her slender torso led to a slim waist before her hips flared. There were fingerprint bruises on those hips from their exploits.

He hissed when she gripped his dick and fit it at her entrance. She sank down over him, enveloping his length in her wet, quivering heat. Her cunt rippled around his dick and damn near made his eyes cross.

When he was fully embedded, she held still, staring into his eyes, drawing the moment out until he could barely stand it. His breath whooshed out in a rush when she canted her hips slowly, drawing his length out until only the tip remained before she rocked her hips and took him deep.

He groaned, and finally clasped her hips. Her hands were like hot brands on his chest as she rode him, undulating and thrusting her gorgeous hips to take him in. He fucking loved watching his cock disappear in her pretty pussy. Those pink labia lips surrounded him.

He thrust up, meeting her downward strokes. Her tits bounced enticingly, making him hunger to suck the buds into his mouth.

But it was her face that captured the brunt of his attention. He'd thought her beautiful since the moment they met. But with pleasure riding her features, she was fucking gorgeous. Her head was tossed back. Long, dark hair spilled over her shoulders and down her back. Moans spilled from her lips. Her eyes were slitted, with ecstasy filling their depths.

She seemed to be drawing it out as she rode him, like she didn't want it to end. Except he knew he wouldn't last forever.

Gripping her hips, he attempted to increase the pace. She locked her legs around his waist, kept him imprisoned and his pace slow—achingly, mind-numbingly slow, until he wondered if he could die from sex with her.

"Faster," he demanded through gritted teeth.

"I'm in charge now."

The woman seemed to know exactly what to say to unleash his inner beast. He was bigger, stronger, and a fucking Dominant. He didn't take orders, he gave them. It was time Eve learned.

With ease, he lifted her off his cock and lap. Eve gasped and sputtered, "What are you doing?"

He rose, bending her forward until that killer ass of hers was up in the air in front of him. He spread her legs, giving him clear access to her weeping cunt. He plunged a finger in her pussy and was rewarded with her moan.

"As much as I loved the blow job and am looking forward to another, we do this my way, honey. You don't command me. Understand?"

"Please, Duncan." She tried to wriggle her hips and thrust on the inserted finger.

But he wasn't letting her. He wanted her to understand the kind of man she had given herself to—one who fully intended to run through every one of the fantasies he'd had of her over the last few weeks.

"Who is in charge of this pussy?" He added a second finger to her greedy cunt.

"You are."

"That's right." He smacked her butt, and felt her clench around his fingers. "You liked that, didn't you?"

"Yes," she whispered brokenly.

He did it a second time. When he felt her cunt ripple and heard her breathy moan, he almost busted a nut. Someone was submissive, and liked to walk on the kinky side of things. Although, from her surprised gasps, he doubted any lover had ever spanked her before.

He would be the first. Not this morning, but soon.

Duncan pulled his finger out, dragging it through her crease to her puckered rosette. "Ever had a man here, honey?"

"No." Her breath shuddered out.

"Relax. I won't take your pretty ass this morning." But the thought of being the first man in her back channel had him grabbing her hips and thrusting his shaft deep.

She curled her back like a cat as she moaned. "Duncan."

With Eve on all fours, he set a blistering pace. The sound of flesh slapping flesh competed with the sound of nature waking. He plowed her hot flesh, loving the slick glide as she squeezed him on every thrust.

He bent over her back, needing to get closer, needing to fuck as if his life depended on it. Grunting, he pummeled her taut hole. He fucked her hard enough that they moved to the ground, until she was lying flat on her belly.

He wrapped his arms around her, gripping her neck. He slammed into her again and again. Feeling the fluttering spasms of her orgasm approaching, he let himself go, pounding into her relentlessly. His thrusts grew more rapid, all control lost.

At the first spasming clasp of her cunt, she cried out as she climaxed.

That was all it took to hurtle him over the ledge. He thrust, plunging deep as the pleasure electrified his spine. The jolt lengthened his shaft. His balls drew up taut.

On the next thrust, he came, filling the condom with his spunk. And there was a part of him that wished he was filling her cunt with it. Marking her as his.

Which was asinine. He didn't get attached to women, he thought as he stilled. But then she turned her head and nuzzled her face against his neck. He took her lips in a scorching tangle of tongue and teeth, knowing deep down that they weren't done with each other. That he was having thoughts he never did where women were concerned.

Because he wanted to keep her.

15

*E*ve shivered as she dressed, donning the same jeans she had worn all weekend. She could smell the fire Duncan had started in the firepit in order to cook their breakfast. She pressed a palm over her belly at the mere thought of him.

Last night had exceeded her expectations.

When she'd made her move, she had figured they would have sex, each get that happy glow at the conclusion, and that would be the end of it. But what she had received instead had been a night full of carnal indulgences, each act more wicked and pleasurable than the last. Her body felt well used and sore.

Thinking back, Eve realized she had never had that much sex in a single night. She had never climaxed that many times.

And it was all because of Duncan.

He touched her, and she was a goner. Every. Single. Time.

Once had not been enough. In between their bouts of

lovemaking, she had slept curled at his side with his arms around her. She had never felt so safe.

And heaven help her, but she wanted more. More sexy nights spent in his arms, more kinetically charged lovemaking, more kisses and climaxes, and everything in between. They hadn't discussed seeing each other beyond last night. Would he even be open to it?

Uncertain about the path forward, she donned her coat before opening the tent.

"Coffee is ready. Eggs are almost ready if you want to get the plates together."

Even though they were outside, it was rather homey and domestic with him cooking breakfast. "Sure. There should be a few more scones in the bear bag too, if you'd like."

"I wouldn't turn them down." He cast her a heated glance from his spot beside the fire.

She felt his look all the way to her toes. "After breakfast, what's on the agenda for today?"

"You get to learn how to break down camp and remove all traces of our stay. We want to have as little of an impact on the surrounding environment as possible. Then we'll hike back to my truck once everything's in order."

She nodded as she served up the scones and cut the last apple in half. "Oh. So, the weekend is over then."

Hiding her face, she tried not to be disappointed that their weekend was up. That by noon, they would be returning to their regularly scheduled programs. She couldn't stop the ache in her chest at the thought of never touching him again.

"Only if you want it to be."

She sucked in a breath and swiveled in his direction, needing to see his face. Too afraid to hope, she whispered, "What are you saying?"

"That, as crazy as it sounds after last night, I want more." He handed her a plate now heaped with eggs.

Sitting on the log by the fire, she teased him. "How much more can we do? We did everything."

His eyes hooded seductively. "Oh honey, we've barely scratched the surface."

"And it would just be for sex?" She didn't want to push him into something he didn't want. Hell, she was insane for wanting more than simply sex. But the thing was, even with the short bursts of sleep in between all the sexual aerobatics last night, she had slept better entwined in his arms than she had in the last year.

And he was making her feel—at the precise moment when she had begun to wonder if she was dead inside because of everything she had been through in the past year.

"No. It wouldn't be simply sex, and you know it. As much as I would like to deny that there's more going on here, I can't. I won't lie to you, Eve. Honesty is a big deal for me. I'm not a man who looks for relationships. I've never felt they were worthwhile or believed in the institution of them. I've always been more for the occasional hookup than anything deep and meaningful. But with you, I find I want more."

She swallowed the lump in her throat. Could she give him what he wanted when she was lying to him, to everyone really, about who she was?

Duncan took a seat beside her, holding his plate. "You don't have to answer me right away. You can take some time to think about it if you need to. But I think you know that whatever this is between us, we're not done yet."

Warnings blared in her mind. Agreeing to extend relations with him would only end badly when she had to leave. All she would end up doing was opening herself up to heartache when the time came.

And yet, the fact that her breath caught in her throat the moment she spied him by the fire spoke volumes. She had it bad where he was concerned. She wanted him beyond a few quick tumbles. Which was why she was making the offer before her brain realized what she was doing. "Would you like to have dinner at my cabin tonight?"

Duncan cupped her chin with his free hand, and rubbed his thumb over her bottom lip. He leaned down and brushed his mouth over hers. It was just a light press of lips that rocked her to her very foundation, because it spoke of care, of the potential, inherent in his touch. And for the first time since leaving her home and name behind, she wanted to confide in him, hand him all her problems, and lean.

The kiss was over before it had really begun. "Dinner would be great. Eat, before the eggs get cold. We've got a lot to do once breakfast is done."

They sat side by side on the log and plowed through the meal. Until she took that first bite, she hadn't realized how hungry she was. But it shouldn't be a surprise given all the sexual aerobatics. They had burned tons of calories.

Eve tried to think about what she should cook that evening as she polished off her scone.

It was easier to focus on potential meals than on the fear that she was making a big mistake by letting this relationship with Duncan continue. It wasn't that she was a commitment-phobe—far from it. She had always thought by the time she was thirty, she would at least be married and starting a family. It was what she wanted most, the closeness of family, where she could look at them and say these were her people, and where she fit.

She believed that was why she had been utterly blind where Silas had been concerned. She had been lonely, so desperate to find her person, that she had overlooked the red flags.

When they had finished eating, they worked together to clean up after the meal. Then they began storing and repacking all the gear. It was surprising how much fit into their packs. But it also left Eve with a list of things to look into picking up. Worst case scenario, if Trevor found her, she could head deeper into the wilderness. Maybe find a cabin off the grid or move around camping from place to place until she lost him completely.

The last part of the gear they broke down was the tents. Duncan walked her through the proper way to fold and store the tents so they fit perfectly in their backpacks.

"Good job. Let's make a sweep of the site, make sure we got everything, and then we'll head out."

"Okay." She nodded. Leaving her pack on the

ground, she went in the opposite direction, scanning the ground and area for anything they might have missed.

She came up empty. He did too. She shouldered her pack.

"Ready?" he asked.

"Yeah, let's go. I'm dying for a shower," she said, trying to ease the sudden tension, not sure how the relationship between them would proceed. It made her uneasy because he could hurt her. She never thought he would in the physical sense of things. It was more that her inexperienced, bruised heart had been battered by life with such intensity, she wasn't sure if she would survive another broken heart.

Duncan laughed as they located the trail back to the main road. "It's only been two days."

"And I'm used to showering every day." She didn't care if that made her sound high maintenance or not.

"In the Navy, anytime we were on mission, it could be a full week or more before we had a chance to get clean."

"Ew, really?"

"Yeah. It's part of the life. On base, showers were available. But out in the middle of the Afghan or Iraqi desert, forget it."

"I hadn't considered that. It couldn't have been easy.'

"You got used to it because it was part of the job, just like sleeping on the ground in your gear with your loaded gun at your side."

"But you knew that going in because of your dad, right? Did you live on military bases?"

"We did while my parents were together. Dad was

overseas on deployment most of the time. They split when I was nine. After that, I would only spend time at the base with him whenever he was on leave."

"I'm sorry. That couldn't have been easy."

"No, it wasn't at the time."

"Where are they now?"

"Mom died while I was deployed in Afghanistan a decade ago—ovarian cancer. Dad keeps in touch. He's retired and living in Florida with his new wife, Carly. I've only met her once, but she seems to make my dad happy."

"I'm sorry about your mom. It had to be hard to lose her that way."

"It was, but I've made my peace with it. She was a good mom and didn't deserve to have it end that way. Being in the military saved me, though. If I had been here, I likely would have drunk myself into an early grave."

"Well, I'm glad you didn't." Eve understood what that kind of loss could do to a person.

"What about you? Where's your family at?"

"Only child, and my parents are both gone."

Duncan stopped on the trail and clasped her arm, waiting until she looked at him before asking, "How old were you?"

"Twenty-two. They were driving, taking a road trip to North Carolina to stay in a bed and breakfast for their anniversary. The driver of a tractor trailer had a heart attack. His eighteen-wheeler crossed the median and hit them head on. They were killed on impact."

"Oh honey." He pulled her into his arms. "I'm sorry.

What about the rest of your family? Aunts, uncles, grand-parents?"

"Both of my parents were only children. When they died, the only one remaining was my grandma on my mom's side of things, and she was in a nursing home with dementia."

"And you've been on your own ever since, I take it." He pulled back, staring down at her.

"Yeah. The holidays tend to be the worst part of it. When everyone else is getting together with family and loved ones."

"You won't be alone this year," he said, resuming their trek.

"I won't, huh?"

"It's only a few weeks away. I figure you could spend it with Sampson and me. We grill steaks, watch football. It will be fun."

The offer surprised her, because from the way he was talking, this thing between them wasn't a fly by night experience. He was acting like he was in it for the long haul, whatever that looked like. Her heart ached with how much she wanted that. How much she wanted the comfort of having him guarding her back, making her feel safe, and cherished.

The wall around her heart cracked. She was going to have to be extremely careful because if he kept saying things like that, she would never let him go.

The three of them arrived at Duncan's truck shortly after eleven. The sun was high in the sky, warming things up considerably. After stowing the packs in the truck bed, he held the passenger side door open for her, and gave her a little boost up into the seat.

He drove her straight to her house. "Duncan, I need to check out at reception and get my truck," she protested, although the sight of her cabin made her want to rush inside, strip out of her dirty clothes, and stand beneath the hot shower spray until she got warm.

Duncan pulled his phone out, punched a few buttons on the smartphone, and then put it up to his ear. "Hey Mike, it's Duncan. Just want to let you know I'm dropping Ms. Carruthers off at her cabin. If you don't mind doing the checkout without her present? Uh-huh, okay, thanks."

He hung up the phone and shot her a knowing glance.

"Done. You're all checked out. Mike will put the receipt in your mailbox in the office. We can retrieve your truck later."

Sighing, she got out of the truck, realizing that he wasn't going to back down on this. "Fine. I'll see you in a few hours then."

He grabbed her pack and walked toward her. "Who says I'm leaving?" He ushered her toward the front door, with Sampson hot on their heels.

"Duncan, I need to take a shower—"

"So do I. Who says we can't do it together?" He took her keys from her hand and opened the front door. "Unless you're tired of me already?"

Sampson bolted inside, making himself at home on the couch by the time they entered.

It wasn't that at all. Eve had been hoping for a few

hours to think. But Duncan stepped into her, tugged her close, and nibbled along her jawline until he reached her ear. Seductively, he murmured, "Come on, honey, be naughty with me. Let me wash every nook and cranny and make you come screaming my name."

He nipped her earlobe. She shivered as the heat rose in her belly and spilled outward. She was powerless against his animal magnetism. A simple touch, and she was aroused beyond measure.

"How could I possibly refuse such an offer?"

"You can't." He tugged her inside, shutting the door behind him.

He was right. She couldn't. And it might have worried her, except the moment they were inside, he tossed the pack onto the floor and kissed her, obliterating every sentient thought in her head.

He had, in short order, taken over the scope of her world.

16

They disrobed on the way to the bathroom—dropping his shirt on the floor there, tossing her bra in the direction of the chest of drawers. But Eve paid no heed to where it all fell, because Duncan was kissing her with that uber dominance of his, and it commanded every ounce of her attention.

Heat burned a path through her body every place he touched. By the time they reached her small, stand-up shower, her pussy was slick with dew.

Duncan pulled her into the shower, closing the door behind them. He locked them in together and started the water, cranking the temperature up. They stood beneath the hot spray. Duncan ran his hands up and down her back as they kissed, a hot tangle of tongue and lips, each kiss more potent than the last.

His erection pressed into her belly, and she wanted him inside her, right here, right now. But before she could grip his cock, he moved back, grabbing the soap and her loofah. He lathered the soap on thick before he began washing her body.

He started with her chest, paying particularly close attention to her breasts. After he'd rinsed the suds off, he swooped down and sucked a turgid nipple into his mouth. Her head fell back on a gasp. His tongue lashed at the bud with fervor. She gripped his shoulders for purchase as he abraded each one with his tongue, lips, and teeth. He placed bites all over the mounds, some hard enough to leave marks behind.

And she didn't know why, but she found the thought of wearing his brand, proof of their lovemaking, oddly erotic, and a huge turn on.

"Duncan," she moaned when he bit her straining nipple to the point of pain. The sharp nip sent a volt of erotically charged tingles from her nipple to her groin.

"Hush, now. I'm not done washing you yet."

He resumed washing her body, scrubbing down her torso and over her belly. She bit her bottom lip as he neared the promised land. But he stopped just shy of entering.

He bent down, lifting her right foot up slightly, and scrubbed her calf, up over her knee to her thigh. Still, as he neared the spot that would send her hurtling into ecstasy, he stopped just before he reached her pussy.

He repeated the gesture with her other leg. His hands were like magic, massaging out all the aches as he cleaned two days' worth of dirt and grime from her body. As his hands neared the apex of her thighs, she quivered, beyond aroused.

But he stopped. Again.

"Duncan," she whimpered.

He dropped to his knees. "Lift your foot, honey, and place it on the bench there."

Her core tightened. Keeping her gaze on his, she brought the leg he had indicated up, and rested her foot on the bench.

The move parted her thighs wide, and gave him clear access to her pussy. He cast her a heated glance before he brought the loofah up, rubbing it through her folds. She hissed as he used the sponge to clean her delicate flesh. When he'd rinsed the suds off, he leaned forward and drew his tongue along her crease.

She whimpered as he teased her clit, circling the engorged bud without actually touching it. He brought his fingers into the mix, stroking her labia, dipping his finger into her entrance and retreating.

Just when she wanted to beg him for more, he latched his mouth around her clit, sucking hard on the nub as he inserted two fingers in her sheath. Her head fell back against the tile as the hot spray beat down a steady stream of water.

He pulsated his tongue against the bud. She slid her fingers into his hair and held on as he lashed at her flesh.

He curled his thrusting fingers on each retreat, rubbing against her G-spot with each plunge. Her cries of pleasure filled the shower.

He bit down on her clit. The orgasm took her by surprise, shattering her as the pleasure made her knees wobble.

"Oh god!" she screamed, her moans filling the space.

He continued to lick her flesh until the spasms

subsided. With a last kiss on her belly, he rose to his full height.

She held out her hand. "My turn."

He handed the loofah over. She added more soap. "Turn around."

Duncan shifted, giving her his back. She started at his neck and impossibly wide shoulders, stroking and caressing his flesh wherever she moved the loofah. She ran delicate fingers over his scars before placing a kiss over them.

His body was battle hardened. She loved the way his muscles rippled and clenched beneath her touch. She moved lower, running her hands over the taut muscles in his ass, toying with the two dimples right above his butt. She leaned in, teasing both with her tongue, then bent lower and nipped his ass cheek. She was rewarded with a sharp hiss.

She washed the backs of his thick thighs, his knees, and the back of his calves before rising. She ordered, "Turn."

When he did as she asked, she felt lightheaded. This big, powerful man was giving her full rein with his stellar body. Did he know how much that turned her on? That even though she had experienced an orgasm a short time before, her body was primed and ready for more wicked lovemaking?

As he faced her, she focused on his body. If she looked into his eyes, she would lose her train of thought. And she wanted to continue exploring his body, since she could see it. His shoulders were so powerful, and she marveled at the taut lines. Nibbled at his collarbone. She traveled lower to his well-defined pecs with dark whorls of hair on them. She moved the sponge over them, enjoying the way the flat disks of his nipples hardened at her touch.

Leaning in, she tongued one of the buds. Duncan groaned, and his cock jolted against her belly. She did it a second time, enjoying the flavor of his skin. She sucked on his nipple, hard enough, his hands grasped the sides of her head.

She released him and looked up at him through her lashes.

His eyes were dark, liquid pools of lust. She felt a quiver low in her belly. If she didn't want to finish what she had started, she would stop and let him take over. But she wanted this, wanted to drive him as crazy as he did her.

She moved to his other nipple, administering the same torturous treatment, enjoying the way he trembled at her touch.

When had any man ever trembled for her?

None. Never. And it twisted her up inside. But she shoved the thought aside, returning to her exploration of his body, descending to his washboard abs and obliques. His victory lines were solid muscle and well defined. She traced them... with her tongue.

But she ignored his erection.

She knelt at his feet, mimicking his caresses as she washed his calves first, then his knees and thighs. She kissed the scars on his leg, the bullet hole a puckered scar that made her realize just how dangerous his life had been.

Until, finally, on her knees, she washed his cock and balls. Rolling his heavy testes in her fingers, she watched his reactions through her lashes. When his dick was thoroughly clean, she gripped him by the base, and ran her tongue from root to tip.

"Oh, fuck. Suck it, honey."

She laved her tongue over the crown, sliding the tip around the mushroom ridge to the sound of his groans before she finally closed her lips around the head and sucked his shaft into her mouth.

His hands slid into her hair as she sucked him, bobbing her head as she moved her mouth up and down his broad cock. She had never really thought that giving blow jobs were hot. But with Duncan's dark gaze studying the way his shaft disappeared in her mouth, it was one of the hottest things she had ever done. She loved the way he looked at her, the way he felt in her mouth. His salty flavor washed over her tongue, and she moaned as she deep-throated him. Her sex pulsated with need.

Duncan wrenched her head back, pulling her mouth off his dick.

"Enough. I need to fuck that pussy. Let's shut the water off and dry off."

She rose, and staid his hand on the water valve. "No. I need you. Right now."

"Honey, I forgot to bring a condom in with us," he explained with a pained expression, like he didn't want to stop.

"I'm on birth control, and I'm clean. You don't need one."

Duncan's expression appeared fucking thrilled at the

thought, although there was a side dish of hesitancy accompanying it. "Are you sure?"

She had never been so sure of anything in her life. It was the first time in her life she would be with a man without one. But she wanted that closeness with him, feeling him skin to skin without any barrier. Nodding, she murmured, "Yes. Take me. Right here, right now."

Duncan took her at her words. He yanked her into his arms, and spun her around until her back was pressed against the tile. "Put your arms around my neck."

The order slid over her like warm melted butter. She gripped his shoulders tight. He lifted her up, wrapping her legs around his waist. The move put his cock against her folds, and they both groaned.

He shifted his torso, fit the head of his cock at her entrance, then demanded, "Open your eyes and look at me."

Eve hadn't realized that she had closed them. She lifted her lids. The moment their gazes connected, he thrust, with a firm roll of his hips, seating himself inside her to the hilt. She moaned, her eyelids heavy with the cascade of pleasure blazing through her body.

She held on as he began to move, stroking deep inside her until it felt like they were one being. He canted his hips, plunging deep. The steady rhythm beat against her hips.

She didn't want to fall for this man. But she could sense that she was standing on a ledge, overlooking an abyss, and all it would take was a little shove to send her hurtling over.

Dammit. No. She wouldn't allow it.

She chided herself. Just because he believed they could have a real relationship, deep down, she knew that in the end, they didn't have a chance. Not when he expected honesty. It was the one thing she couldn't give him. Her lies would catch up with her eventually if she was here long enough. And when he discovered them, he would hate her.

He used the tile wall for support as his pace quickened. He pummeled her cunt. The feel of him inside her without the latex was incredible. Being skin to skin made the sex even more intense.

Right here, as he buried his face in the crook of her neck and hammered her pussy, nothing but the two of them existed. The world could be falling to ruin, and they wouldn't notice. And she wouldn't trade this moment for anything else in the world.

"Duncan," she whimpered, feeling the first flutters of her orgasm approach.

"That's it, honey. Come for me." He reached between them, and pinched her clit.

The move set her off like a rocket, launching her body off the planet as she quaked. Duncan plunged with a hearty groan. His cock jolted in her spasming pussy. And for the first time in her life, a man came inside her without a condom. His warm semen flooded her sex and set off another round of spasms so that she was clinging to him, wailing his name.

He held her there, against the tile with the water beating down on them and his face buried against her neck for long enough, she started to drift.

He moved first. She lifted her heavy lids. Her heart

rolled over and exposed its soft underbelly. In this moment, she knew unequivocally that she could fall for him.

He kissed her sweetly, gently, as if she were precious to him. Tears pricked the corners of her eyes because she knew if he ever discovered her lies, that would be the end of it.

Tenderly, he helped her onto her feet, and proceeded to wash away the traces of their lovemaking—gently this time, with care, until she began to wonder if she hadn't already lost part of herself to him.

By the time they shut the water off, it ran cold. But she didn't care as he bundled her up in a thick towel. All she cared about was soaking up as much time with him as possible. It would make the lonely nights to come bearable—or so she hoped.

"Are you hungry?" she asked as they left the bath behind.

"Famished."

And she could tell by the look in his eyes that he wasn't simply talking about food.

17

On Wednesday afternoon, Duncan strode into the hotel for his meeting with Amber and his team. He checked around the lobby, searching for a certain maid he couldn't seem to keep off his mind. In a short amount of time, she had become an addiction. She was in his blood—and, he feared, in his heart and soul too.

Any time he suggested a more permanent arrangement, she hemmed and hawed, while telling him that they simply should take the relationship one day at a time. That, since it was new, of course they were treating each other's bodies like an all you can eat buffet.

Eve was the first woman in years to turn his head, and none who had come before her had ever done so in quite this way. Whereas with most women, the ardor would be cooling by now simply with the sheer volume of sex, this time around, it didn't seem to matter that he had left her bed a few short hours ago because he wanted her again—now, and, he feared, always. Instead of diminishing, his appetite for Eve had only grown.

What was more, he couldn't help but feel the rightness of it. She fit him in ways no other woman ever had—when he touched her, he was home. She was independent and fierce, spoiled Sampson rotten to the point where Duncan might have to compete with his damn dog for her affections, and he couldn't get enough of her.

In the days since taking her to bed, he had slowly begun testing her response to his dominance. She had not batted an eye when he had restrained her hands above her head last night. If anything, her moans had increased tenfold. He'd known she was submissive.

And he planned to take her deeper, push her boundaries, and discover just how far he could take her tonight.

He had reserved Cabin X this evening, the site of their first kiss. He remembered the swift punch of lust he had felt, seeing her among the BDSM furniture. Tonight would be a test of her willingness to submit to him.

He couldn't fucking wait.

Duncan didn't catch a glimpse of her in the halls as he made his way up to the conference room. With winter fully setting in, they weren't doing overnights for the next two months. It got too damn cold. Subzero temperatures would put guests in the hospital—or worse.

This meant that, for the next little while, he would do the daily outdoor survival for those who'd booked. On days when he didn't have outdoor survival sessions booked, he filled in where needed—either with the horses or cattle, or sometimes he filled in with Lincoln, doing repairs and maintenance. They were assigning Matt and Eli to other departments until the spring.

Duncan schooled his features. While he wasn't at all

ashamed that he was dating Eve, he wasn't in the mood for his buddies' teasing. Although, he hadn't taken her on an actual date. That was something he needed to rectify at the soonest opportunity.

In the conference room, Maverick, Noah, Matt, and Eli sat around the long wooden table in black leather chairs. The conference table was large enough, it could seat twenty of them at a time if needed. The only one missing from their meeting was Amber. Mav and Noah were born and bred cowboys and it showed in their bearing. They were most comfortable in the stables or on horseback, looking out of place in the office setting. Noah had removed his Stetson. It rested on the table beside him. Mav left his hat on. Matt had recently adopted wearing a cowboy hat. He liked to say the black Stetson made the female tourists go gaga. But Eli was like Duncan in that he wasn't about to give up his ballcap for a Stetson—not anytime soon, anyhow.

Eli smirked as Duncan took a seat. His eyes danced with mirth as he leaned back in his chair and studied him.

"Something on your mind, Eli?"

But Eli didn't address him, instead he said to the rest of the fellas, "You guys see our good friend Duncan over here, out with the new maid?"

How the fuck did he know about that? Not that Duncan was trying to keep their relationship a secret, but they hadn't exactly gone public with it yet. He'd been thinking the New Year's Eve shindig the hotel put on in the ballroom would be soon enough for that.

Every head in the room turned his way. Maverick wore a shit-eating grin and commented, "Is that right?"

Duncan grimaced. He knew Mav's little dig was payback for ribbing him over Bianca earlier this year. Shrugging his shoulders, he cast a blasé stare at his friends. "I don't know what Eli is talking about."

"He can play it cool all he wants. Last night, on my drive home, I passed by the little maid's cabin, thinking I would be all neighborly and shit. And what do I see, but this guy standing on her porch, with the little maid wrapped around him like a pretzel. They were kissing each other." Eli chuckled and clapped, as if he was proud of Duncan for making a move.

Shit, Duncan hadn't thought anyone would see them. When he had made it to Eve's place last night, she practically vaulted into his arms. Good thing Eli hadn't stayed to watch the show, because it had gotten wild fast after that. Eve and Duncan had barely made it inside her cabin —and they only had because it was cold as all get out. The last thing he wanted to do was freeze his nuts off, literally. Instead of continuing to deny their relationship, he shifted, and took a direct approach. "And your point?"

"It's serious then?" Noah asked, his brows almost disappearing beneath his hairline.

Yes, it was serious. Each day, Duncan became a little more attached, a little more desperate to make Eve his in every way that mattered. But he wasn't ready to give voice to those feelings to Eve yet, which meant he definitely wasn't close to admitting his feelings to these knuckleheads. "I'm not sure what our relationship is, just yet, and I would appreciate it if you would butt out until I do."

"Oh man, he's serious about this one." Matt leaned

back in his chair. "You ever remember Duncan being serious about a woman?"

Eli shook his head with a smarmy laugh. "Nope. Not a single one in all the years we served together."

Noah laughed. "I'll be damned, she must be something to take down the indomitable Duncan Bowers. Can't wait to meet her."

"You're one to talk." Duncan shot Noah a glower. "You married the nanny."

At the mention of his wife, Noah smiled. "Hey, I am one hundred percent loving every day since Morgan came into my life. I wouldn't change a thing. If this woman does it for you, why wouldn't you grab a hold?"

That was what Duncan was beginning to think when it came to Eve: that he wanted to hold on to her for one hell of a lot longer than a few hot, sweaty nights. In fact, he had even begun thinking about marriage and children —which, in the past, would have sent him running for the hills.

But not with Eve. Hell, with Eve, it felt right.

She had wriggled her way past his armor. And he was sinking fast. The most startling thing was that he didn't want to hold back. He wanted to explore her depths, and see what they could be together. Duncan wanted to go all in.

And while that thought terrified him, he could no longer imagine his life without her in it in some fashion. She had slowly begun winding him around her pinky. Even though, deep down, he knew she was keeping secrets from him.

There was something more about the person she'd

trusted that had backfired. The guy who had hurt her. The one Duncan would love five minutes alone with for even looking in her direction, let alone hurting her.

She mattered to him. How much—that remained to be seen.

"Well, I think it's about damn time you dated something other than your hand," Eli commented, and garnered laughs from the room.

"She is a looker, I will give you that. I think it's great you've got your boxers all twisted up over her," Maverick added with a lopsided grin.

"I've not met her yet. But then, I rarely get to the main hotel. How long has she been working here?" Noah asked the room in general.

"Since right before Thanksgiving," Matt stated. "And the lieutenant beat me and Eli to the punch, since we were each going to take a shot at her."

Noah whistled. "You move fast."

"And how long was it after you hired Morgan to be your nanny before you slept with her?" Duncan asked pointedly.

"Touché." Noah nodded. "Sometimes, when it's right, length of time knowing someone doesn't matter."

"Yeah, and from the liplock those two were in, I would say that wasn't the first time, either," Eli stated, wiggling his brows like the show he had witnessed had been hot.

"Well, she was the only guest on his camping trip this past weekend," Matt added.

Duncan wanted to clean Matt's clock as brows went up in surprise around the room. The fucker. Maverick tossed his head back and laughed like it was the funniest thing he had heard in a week of Sundays.

And that was when the boss walked in. Finally. It meant they could move on with the meeting, and stop discussing Duncan's love life.

"What's so funny, gentlemen?" Amber asked, taking her seat at the head of the conference table. She was dressed smartly in a dark green suit and black, knee-high stiletto boots.

"Only that our man Duncan, eternal bachelor that he is, has been seeing the new maid." Eli wiggled his brows.

Duncan was going to kill the fucker for bringing it up in front of the boss.

Amber's lips compressed into a thin line. "I see. If we can get to the business at hand, and not which flavor of the month Duncan has decided to play with?"

"He's not playing with her. Seems to me, he's quite serious about the new maid," Matt stated.

"Be that as it may, we have a lot of ground to cover, and a short time to do it. I would appreciate it if we could get this done, as I have two more meetings today alone." Amber gave them all a cool glare.

Duncan liked Amber. She was phenomenal at her job. Better than her brother in some aspects. If her brother Colt was still at the helm, he would have added to the ribbing, not shut it down.

"Sure thing, Amber." Maverick nodded.

"Great. Okay, talk to me about the schedule," Amber ordered.

Duncan, Maverick, and Noah took turns explaining the schedule the three of them had worked out for Matt and El, with Matt and Eli commenting from time to time, particularly when Amber asked them a question.

By the time the meeting ended, Duncan was looking forward to the next few months. It was a change in his routine. None of the work was difficult, even though some was physically taxing. Nor did he really relish the idea of mucking out stalls, but it was still loads better than some of the shitholes he had been dropped into overseas.

Before everyone headed out the door, Amber spoke up. "Duncan, could you hang back a minute?"

"Sure thing." He glared at Eli on his way out the door. That guy loved stirring shit up. Made Duncan want to box the dude's ears for thinking it was all right to go saying all the shit within hearing distance of the boss.

Once they were alone, Amber folded her hands together on the table and shot him a stony glance. "While there is no company policy against employees seeing one another, I'm going to ask that you be careful with Eve. I like her. She's a good worker, and a good fit for this hotel. She's smart and eventually, if she's here long enough, I have some other ideas I would like to present to her."

"I'm always careful. This thing between Eve and me is still in its infancy. I had no intention of telling anyone about it yet. The only reason it was even brought up is because Eli saw us together the other night. But I can promise you that I won't let it get in the way of her work, or mine."

"That's good. Yet you sound frustrated. Anything I can do to help?"

Duncan chewed over saying something before he

admitted, "She's hiding something. There was a guy who hurt her. She won't give me the details. The thing is, every instinct I have tells me she's running from this guy, that he might be after her. But she's playing it very close to the chest. When I asked her about it the other night, she clammed up real quick."

"I see. And she's not opening up to you?" Amber tilted her head. "Because I thought the same when she interviewed with me. That she was running from something. She doesn't jump as much as she used to, though, so that is a good thing."

He remembered the way Eve's nerves had gotten the better of her when he had startled her. Whoever the guy was, he had done a number on her. "I'm getting bits and pieces, which is why I know there was a guy she trusted who hurt her. I don't know in what way, whether it was physical or not. But since you mentioned it, maybe you could befriend her. It's not like she has any female friends. Perhaps you might be able to get her to open up and talk about it a bit. It worries me."

"It's that bad, you think?"

"Absolutely. She's been through trauma. There's no doubt about that, after seeing her nerves when someone inadvertently sneaks up on her, and the nightmares she has most nights. But I'm worried if I push her on it..."

"She'll shut you out," Amber finished the sentence for him, the light of understanding in her gaze.

"Yes. Precisely. And I'm going to tell you something I didn't want to admit to those knuckleheads: I'm playing the long game with Eve. I would appreciate it if you kept that between us."

A grin spread over Amber's face. "Well, that changes things, doesn't it? Don't worry, I won't revoke your tough man card just for having feelings."

"Thanks."

"As far as Eve is concerned, I'll see what I can do. Although, you could always use those Dom skills to get her to talk."

He'd thought the same thing, especially if tonight at Cabin X went well. "What do you know about Dom skills?"

"More than any of you guys using Cabin X realize," Amber stated coolly with a shake of her head.

Fair enough. She was a grown woman who knew her own mind. While Colt might have laid down the law that his sister was off limits, Duncan doubted there was much that went on at the ranch she didn't know. "I don't want to use that method unless I have no other option. I would rather she came to me on her own with it. For me, as a Dom, it's about trust, building it along with the foundation for a future."

"I see your point. Perhaps I could invite her to Grace's baby shower this weekend, and it could be a team effort."

Relief flooded him. "Thanks, Amber. I appreciate it."

"Good. Now, I've got to skedaddle. I've got a marketing meeting in ten."

"I'll walk you out." He rose from his seat, wondering what it was going to take for Eve to fully trust him with all her secrets.

18

Skittish energy flowed off Eve as Duncan turned the truck into the driveway for Cabin X, and parked. The lodge was theirs for the night, which meant none of his buddies would stop by to use it. For Eve's first time in a scene, he preferred that it be only the two of them, with no distractions.

"Are you sure you're okay with coming here tonight? I don't want to pressure you to do anything you aren't ready for."

She cast him a tremulous smile. "I am nervous, but only because I've never done anything like this before. But there's also excitement mixed in as well."

He clasped her hand in his and brushed his lips over her knuckles. "I promise you that if there's anything that you don't like, we will stop immediately and switch gears. The biggest part of participating in BDSM is being open and honest with your partner about your likes and dislikes."

Uncertainty flashed through her eyes when he mentioned honesty.

Just what are you hiding, honey?

"I'm sure it will be great. I thoroughly enjoyed all those other things you've done." A pretty blush spread over her cheeks.

She wasn't the only one. He sent her a carnal smirk, caressing her stellar body with his gaze. Even with her body hidden beneath her thick coat, she was a knockout. "That was the tip of the iceberg, honey. Tonight, we're going to go a wee bit farther than that."

"Let's do it." She nodded, her face resolved, with a smattering of eagerness to boot.

She was magnificent. Was it any wonder that she had hooked him right from the start? She ignited his need to protect. He craved to possess her body and soul—and, if he was lucky, maybe even her kind and giving heart.

The scene tonight was not going to involve pain. This first full foray into BDSM for her would be solely about extracting every ounce of pleasure he could wring from her body, and her complete surrender to his dominance.

Exiting his truck, he strode around to the passenger side to collect her. With a possessive hand on her lower back, he escorted her up the steps, typed his entry code in the keypad, and let them inside. As they entered, the lights flickered on automatically.

When they'd constructed the interior of the cabin, they had worked to make the place as self-sufficient and easy to use as possible. They had a list of rules. An online calendar system to reserve the space. A once a month voyeurs and hedonists night—although, since Emmett,

Cole, Maverick, and now Noah, were all engaged or hitched, those nights were dwindling. It was like once they were in a committed relationship, they didn't want to share their partner's form with anyone.

Not that Duncan blamed them, because when it came to Eve, he was downright territorial.

Duncan steered her over to the bench she had been caressing when he'd found her in here last time. She glanced at him with a raised brow and question in her eyes that plainly stated she was skeptically unsure about the coming scene.

"I figured it would be fitting for your first time."

She shook her head and laughed. "Either that, or you're a bit of a sadist."

"Well, you're about to find that one out, aren't you?" He spied the nerves in her eyes. Needing to comfort her, help her to relax so that she could enjoy the evening he had planned, he cupped her face in his hands and kissed her. Her sweet flavor combined with the mint from her toothpaste rolled over his tongue. Tilting her head back, sliding a hand to her nape, he sealed his mouth over hers, and delved deep. She yielded without qualm, clinging to him as he drank from her lips. They were building something important, something that would last. He couldn't push past how right she felt in his arms, as if it was where she belonged, now and forever. When she leaned into him and her body went pliant, he lifted his mouth.

Rubbing his thumb over her bottom lip, he watched her open eyes that were now cloudy with desire, all traces of anxiety eliminated. Her pupils were dilated. The pulse at the base of her neck fluttered wildly. And he knew if he snaked his hand beneath her jeans, he would find her wet.

Sliding his dominance around him like a blanket, he ordered, "I want you to strip everything off. Then I'm going to put you on the bench and restrain you before I make you come, screaming in ecstasy."

Eve nodded. Before he released her, he pressed his lips against her forehead and let her go. She blew out a breath and unzipped her coat. The nerves weren't gone entirely. That would only happen once she'd experienced the scene and understood there was nothing to fear, that she was safe with him.

Duncan knew beyond any doubt that he was sinking fast where Eve was concerned. In a short space of time, she had altered his entire world. And, ironically enough, there was a part of him that felt like the reason he had never considered settling down was because he had known none of the other women had been right for him —until Eve.

He had feelings for her, surprisingly deep ones at that. And for a man who had eschewed commitment, he wasn't quite certain how to handle them or know what he wanted to do with them exactly. All he did know was that he wanted her in his life and his bed nightly.

While she was busy disrobing, he headed over to the armoire with all the supplies. He pulled out the lickgasm device—it was a vibrating sex toy with a silicone tongue at one end that had a small suction cup around it. It simultaneously licked and sucked. And he planned to prop it up against Eve's succulent pussy.

As an afterthought, he also selected a slim butt plug.

Let's see if she likes a bit of anal play tacked on to our session. He had experimented two nights ago by inserting his thumb in her ass while taking her from behind. To say that she had gone a little crazy was the understatement of the century.

She had come apart for him, screaming his name, her pussy clamping down on his dick so hard, the sheer force of her orgasm had toppled him over the edge.

He carted the supplies over to the padded bench, which Eve stood beside in all her naked glory. Lust that he had held in check all day long at the thought of her charged to the forefront like a snarling beast. Need had his dick straining against the confines of his jeans.

"Fuck, you're beautiful. You should always be naked."

The uncertainty fled her gaze, replaced by pleasure at his compliment. "Only if you're naked with me."

"I will be shortly. Don't you worry. Now before I help you up onto the bench, what was the safeword we discussed that, if you use it during our scene, will make everything stop immediately?"

"Red."

"Good. Remember to use it if you need it. Don't be shy or hesitant about it, either."

He laid the supplies on a small table by the bench, and held out his hand.

"Here, I'm going to help you up. I want you to position yourself on your belly and put that sweet ass of yours right here at the end." He patted the bench with his free hand.

He lifted her by her waist and deposited her on top of

the bench, assisting her and helping her arrange her body the way he wanted for maximum access. Once she was in the proper position, with her bottom hanging over the lip of the bench, he began adding restraints. Beginning with her wrists, he slid leather cuffs around the delicate flesh, ensuring that they weren't too tight or would cut off circulation.

He traveled along the length of her body, attaching a leather strap low across her waist to keep her body immobile before he headed on to her supple, smooth legs. Her knees were bent and rested on the padded ledge. Ensuring that they were comfortably placed, he bound her ankles to the bench with leather straps.

Fuck me. She made quite a sexy picture, all bound for his pleasure.

It took every ounce of the considerable control he possessed not to fall on her and rut like a beast. He strolled around the bench, double checking that her restraints weren't too tight. "How are you doing, honey?"

"Good."

"The restraints aren't scaring you?" He was curious because if she enjoyed this session, it made her damn near the perfect woman—for him, at least.

"No... they feel good. I can't describe the sensations other than it turns me on. It's like the moment you finished fastening them, my insides turned molten."

Immense satisfaction speared him at her words. She was born to be submissive, to be his submissive. Eve was chock full of pleasant surprises. "There's nothing wrong with enjoying it." He caressed a hand down the supple lines of her back. "You look fucking sexy as hell, bound this way. My dick aches to feel your sweet pussy squeezing me."

His hands kneaded the globes of her ass and he was rewarded with her blissful sigh.

"I'd be fine with that."

Her admission made his cock jolt. The naughty minx tested his resolve. "I'm sure you would. But tonight isn't going to be a race to the finish line. In fact, by the time I'm done with you, I doubt you will be able to walk."

"Oh," she murmured as he swirled his fingers through her crease, teasing the swollen button of pleasure that had her crying out.

"There's no limit on the number of times you may come. This time, I want you to come as often as you need to. All you have to do is surrender, give me everything, hold nothing back from me."

"Okay." Her breathy sigh had his gut tightening.

Before he used the lickgasm and plug, he yearned for a taste of her. Kneeling down, he swiped his tongue through her slick folds. Her salty sweet musk flavor hit his tastebuds and he groaned. At Eve's sharp gasp, he applied himself, flicking his tongue over her clit, lapping at her cream until it felt like his cock was nigh to bursting and he was rather pissed he wasn't sliding his shaft in her hot channel.

The little sounds Eve made stoked his internal fires. But his focus was on her, on making her first scene the most pleasurable experience possible. He thrust his tongue in her pussy. Using his thumb, he rubbed her clit, needing to push her body over the edge. An orgasm would relax her enough so that he could easily stretch her back channel.

Using his lips, teeth, and tongue, he drove her up into a screaming orgasm, her body trembling in the restraints. Satisfaction flowed through Duncan as he continued his campaign on her delicate flesh.

By the time he was done, he would solidify the trust between them. And then, perhaps, she would feel comfortable enough divulging all her secrets.

19

Oh my God!

Eve floated in an ocean of exquisite bliss. The orgasm ripped through her at lightning speeds. She moaned low in her throat as Duncan lapped at her cream. It was startling how she could feel her body begin to tighten in on itself once more, hurtling her toward another climax.

Surely, he wasn't going to spend the night just giving her oral. Not that she would mind, because the man was particularly skilled in that arena. He knew the right amount of pressure to exert as he fluttered his tongue against her inflamed nub. After a series of dark nips that left her desperate for release, she whimpered when he suctioned hard on her clit, making her eyes roll back in her head.

The man had a magic mouth, and being the sole focus of all that intensity was a heady, world-altering experience.

As he sucked at her bud, his fingers began to draw her

wetness from her pussy to her naughty back channel. She moaned low as he circled the hole with his thumb. He pressed against her entrance and bit down on her clit at the same time. Sensors crossed in her system. Pleasure blasted her body as his thumb slowly thrust inside her ass.

Who knew she would enjoy something this depraved?

It felt wicked and forbidden and by god, it turned her on like nothing else. Her limbs were deluged with lava. She lowered her head at the waves of pleasure bombarding her. Moans spilled from her lips as his thumb delved deeper, stretching her ass. It was painful but it was good pain. Bound like she was, she couldn't move her hips and lessen the intensity. Her pussy pulsed in time with his thrusting thumb in her rear.

When the pleasure abruptly cut off, she whimpered, then hissed as coolness hit her back channel.

"Oh god," she muttered. Duncan penetrated her rear with a long, thick finger, delving deeper than his thumb. It felt depraved. It engulfed her body in flames. She was being incinerated one gliding thrust at a time.

"One of these days, I'm going to fuck you here. It makes me so hard even thinking about it, being the first and only to bury my dick in your ass."

Eve wanted it too. She mewled at the erotic imagery of his cock in her ass as he added a second finger to the first. The pressure burned and was uncomfortable as he stretched her, but it rode that sweet edge between pain and pleasure that was downright irresistible.

"You like the thought of that, don't you? Me fucking your ass."

"Yes." She whimpered the admission. She wanted it now. Wanted to try every single one of his wicked fantasies, along with some of her own. She had never considered herself a sexual being until Duncan. She loved the feel of him inside her, loved the way he touched her and kissed her. Her body relaxed as she adjusted to his fingers thrusting in her back channel.

But then he pressed the envelope and added a third finger into the mix. She bit her bottom lip as the intensity grew. Pleasure coiled in her belly, tightening as he advanced deeper, thrusting his fingers until they were embedded, only to widen and spread them while they were buried. She hissed out a groan. "Oh god."

"Easy, honey, take a deep breath for me. I'm stretching you out a bit before I insert the plug. And then I promise to make you feel so good."

She nodded. "Okay."

She inhaled deeply through her nose, and released the breath. As she did, the burning agony in her ass subsided, transforming into indescribable need. The potency of her craving set her teeth on edge, and made her skin feel three sizes too small. Moisture seeped from her pussy as it pulsed in time with the thrusting digits.

It felt incredible, like there was this wonderland of pleasure just out of her reach. She wanted to grab for it and hold on. She was shaking with need—only a few more deep thrusts, and she knew the orgasm would be unlike any she had experienced before.

But then Duncan withdrew his fingers, torturing her by preventing her release. She protested the lack with a whine. "No. I was so close. Please don't stop."

She didn't care that she was begging.

He playfully smacked her rump. "Greedy wench. I should deny you for that but since it's your first time like this, I'll be magnanimous. Just switching my fingers out for the plug, honey."

He added more lube to her entrance. And then she felt the bulbous, cool silicone press against her rear entrance.

"Deep breaths for me."

She complied, too sexually on edge to do otherwise. Duncan thrust the device in until an inch was inside her, only to retreat and thrust again. Proceeding deeper with each pass, the plug gradually widened in a cylindrical fashion. When the plug was fully inserted, she breathed a sigh of relief. Then her mouth dropped open.

"Oh god, Duncan." She moaned as the vibrations hummed in rippling waves, extending from her ass into her pussy.

Duncan chuckled darkly and massaged her butt. "I thought you might like that."

He rubbed her clit for a moment. The dual sensations turned her world upside down. She wondered if a person could actually die from pleasure. "Give me a minute to get the next part set up. Just rest, and enjoy the vibrations from the plug."

"Yes," she whispered with her eyes closed. Every part of her being was electrified. Even the air moving across it inflamed her over-sensitive skin.

Through a lust-infused haze, she heard Duncan moving around behind her. And then a device was placed up against her clit. Only there was also this hood around it that seemed to seal it in.

Before she could comment on it, the device came to life.

Oh. My. God!

The damn thing mimicked a tongue, flicking back and forth against her already swollen clit. She dropped her head forward on a moan as it not only licked relentlessly at her bud, but began suctioning at her flesh.

"Duncan." She moaned, her jaw open as unintelligible sounds came out.

"I figured you might enjoy the lickgasm."

Enjoy it? Between this thing licking her, hitting that one spot without fail on every pass—the way it suctioned the same flesh was such delicious agony—and the vibrations pulsating in her ass, she was going to be unable to hold her orgasms back. In fact, this much pleasure might be capable of powering her body to the moon and back when she came.

Rough hands tenderly cupped her face. She lifted heavy lids and stared into Duncan's blazing black gaze suffused with hunger. He leaned in, and took her mouth in a hungry, soul-searing kiss that left her breathless.

Their tongues tangled as he deepened the kiss. He sucked her tongue into his mouth. That gesture tipped her body over the ledge into a startlingly powerful climax that had her crying out. He swallowed her cries down with his lips before ending the kiss.

And she thought: now. Now, he would fuck her.

But she was wrong. The erotic torture had barely begun. She watched him strip, revealing his powerful form... and the part of him she had come to adore. His thick cock jutted from his apex, so hard it curved slightly near the head. Her mouth watered as pleasure filled-bursts erupted in her core.

Once he was completely bare, he sauntered over, gripped his cock in his hand and murmured, "Open up, honey. I want that hot little mouth of yours sucking me off."

With her arms restrained and unable to reach for him, she opened her mouth. Her tongue shot out, catching the pearly drop of precum seeping from the crown. Duncan hissed as he pushed inside her mouth.

She moaned around his shaft, sucking him deep until he hit the back of her throat. Breathing through her nose, she bobbed her head, focusing on his pleasure even as the waves of another climax rose within her body.

Duncan held her head in his hands as he began to thrust in her mouth. His grunts and groans made her feel powerful. That she could make this big, strapping, badass man lose control was a heady experience.

That thought, combined with the device licking her clit and vibrations in her bottom set off a chain reaction.

"Mmmm." Her cry was garbled with his cock in her mouth as she came. Hard. And for a long time—until the two sex toys made her ache.

Duncan withdrew his shaft from her mouth, bent forward and claimed her lips in a torrid, passionate kiss that left her breathless for more. "You've done so well, honey."

He moved out of her line of sight. The licking machine was shut off and removed from her pussy. But then the rounded head of his shaft pressed against her swollen entrance. Duncan penetrated her slowly, letting her feel every glorious inch of his broad cock. The plug in her back channel made her sheath much tighter. The dual penetration had lava pouring through her veins.

"Duncan," she breathed, biting her lip as her body reforged itself under his tutelage.

"I know. You feel so fucking good squeezing my dick, honey." His hands clasped her hips. He withdrew until only the tip remained before gliding hilt deep with shuddering force.

She panted at the slow, fierce thrusts. It gave her a chance to feel him, all of him. Her pussy throbbed around his shaft.

Duncan increased the tempo of his thrusts, establishing a steady pace. But he wasn't gentle as he fucked her. She had been in this sexual haze from the start of their little kink session, and she didn't think she would ever come down. It was like they had been made for each other with the kinetic swath of carnal passion enveloping them in their own world.

She mewled as he thrust. His grunts and groans competed with the slap of flesh. She tossed her head back, and moaned.

"That's it, honey. Take your pleasure," he growled, slamming inside her with ferocity as his control began to slip.

Her eyes rolled back in her head as his pounding digs turned downright primal. It was as if he was attempting to imprint himself on her body. But he already had, that first night in the tent. With every kiss, each touch, and every deep stroke, Duncan had not just imprinted himself on her body, he had scorched a fiery path through her heart and soul, laying waste to every man who had come before.

No matter what happened, even if she was forced to leave him, she didn't regret this time with him. And she could only pray that in their time together, she would soak up as many nights as she could to remember and relive.

The dual penetration proved to be too much. Her climax kept building, drawing all the energy into her core, tighter and tighter as he hammered inside her. His fingers dug cruelly into her hips, and would likely leave bruises. But she loved the thought of wearing his marks on her body, proof that he desired her that much, that she made him lose control like that.

"Duncan!" She wailed as the climax ripped through her system. Her ass quaked. Her pussy spasmed around his thrusting member. She trembled and shook at the seismic force of her orgasm.

"Oh fuck, honey," Duncan groaned.

He slammed inside, and his cock jerked as he came, spilling his warm spunk in her quivering channel. His climax set off another round of spasms. She was glad she was bound to the bench, because it kept her from melting into the floorboards as her body floated in a sea of ecstasy.

Dimly, she felt him withdraw. She whimpered at the loss. The buzzing in her rear stopped. And then, with great care, he removed the plug.

She sighed at the buttery sensation in her limbs.

Duncan worked to undo her restraints, massaging each limb back to life as he did so.

"Come on, honey." He lifted her up into his arms and carried her over to a nearby leather couch. Wrapping her in a blanket, he deposited her on the sofa as he cleaned up after their scene.

She drifted, close to the precipice of sleep. A hand on her leg jolted her awake. Her eyes snapped open.

"Easy. I just want to get you dressed, and get you home."

"Okay."

With Duncan's assistance, she donned her jeans, top, and coat. He put her boots on for her when her legs wobbled. When she tried to stand again, he caught her before she slid to the ground.

"I've got you. I won't ever let you fall," he murmured against her forehead.

In that moment, she knew he spoke the truth. That he was the real deal. She might stumble. She might fall. But as long as he was with her, she would never hit the ground. And with that knowledge burning inside her soul, the death grip she'd had on her emotions slackened, and she let go.

Love for this man filled her. It awed her. And it made her realize that she didn't want to run anymore, that he made her want to stick around, come what may.

Duncan carried her out to his truck and deposited her in the passenger seat. "Sleep, honey. I'll take you home."

And she knew he would, because the thing was: with him, she was home.

20

On her next day off, Eve found herself in town, shopping for a last minute baby shower gift for the town doctor, Grace. The invite for the shower had come from her boss, Amber. To say that she had been surprised by the invitation was putting it mildly. But then, she had met Grace a time or two at the hotel— usually when she was there to eat lunch with Amber or her husband, Emmett, who was one of the ranch wranglers.

It was early in the day yet, just past nine in the morning. The baby shower was being held at Amber's house in two hours, so Eve had time to pick up a baby gift and stop by the grocery store.

She found a cute as could be stuffed teddy bear with a plaid bow tie, and a set of onesies for the mom to be before heading to the grocery store.

Duncan was on a camping trip this weekend. Temperatures had shot up enough that he had agreed to the trip. It was likely his last one for the next two months.

She shopped for groceries with him in mind. Over the past week, they had spent every night together. In that time, she had paid attention to the foods he liked. Granted, she was pretty sure the man would eat anything she plunked down in front of him. But there were a few dishes and baked goods which always seemed to make him reach for seconds.

This was why she added ingredients for lasagna to her cart. He loved pasta. A few nights ago, he'd scarfed down two plates of spaghetti with meatballs with unrepentant glee. She figured she would make lasagna, a nice Italian salad on the side, and bake some bread tomorrow that she would turn into garlic bread for the meal.

She couldn't seem to stop the dopey grin from splitting her face, either, as she added items to her cart. Considering their inauspicious meeting, the fact that Duncan was now her lover tickled her to no end.

And while she understood that he was waiting for her to talk to him, tell him what was going on, he hadn't pressed. All he'd said when she'd asked him for more time was that he would wait until whenever she was ready to tell him.

It meant the world to her that he was willing to give her the time and space she needed to get comfortable with him and their relationship.

The errant thought stopped her in her tracks. She was in a relationship. Even more revealing than that, while she'd browsed in the baby store, she had gotten this image. It was of a little boy, with her eyes and his smile. And she yearned to make that image a reality, for the possibility of a future with Duncan. But to do that, she would have to be braver than she'd ever thought she could be and tell him everything, holding nothing back about Trevor, Silas, and her year on the run.

But she didn't know how.

How could she tell a man who prided himself on honesty and valor that she was lying to everyone? That her name wasn't even Eve Carruthers? How could she admit that she had been played for a fool? That, instead of standing her ground and fighting, she had run as far and as fast as she could?

When she had finished shopping, she loaded up her purchases into her truck. As she walked her cart over to the big metal corral, she spied a man leaning against the brick wall of the post office next door. Much of his face was hidden by sunglasses and a black cowboy hat.

Chills raced down her spine. Anxiety spurred her movements. She powerwalked back to her truck, trying to play it cool, as if she was merely in a hurry when it was fear giving her feet wings.

She glanced over her shoulder.

Her heart raced. He was still there—looked like he hadn't moved a muscle. And he was watching her intently.

Spurred into action, she vaulted into the front seat and snapped her seatbelt on. Shoving the key in the ignition, she cranked the engine. Her truck sputtered to life. Pulling out of her parking space, she glanced back toward the post office.

She sucked in a breath.

He was gone. She frantically glanced around, trying to find him. The guy had vanished into thin air.

Leaving the grocery store parking lot, Eve decided to circle town, see if she could find him. It would also confuse him if he was following her at all. She kept an eye on the vehicles behind her, scanning each and every one that passed her for that strange man.

After thirty minutes of driving through town, she turned onto the two-lane highway to head home. The entire drive she spent looking over her shoulder, checking out the trucks and cars behind her.

She didn't breathe easier until she turned onto ranch property, and no one followed her off the highway.

While the guy might have been harmless, it drove the message home that any day, Trevor could appear and rip her away from the life she was building.

What was worse, there were a few minutes on the drive when she'd seriously considered calling Duncan on the SAT phone. It was the only way to reach him on a camping trip. And it was stupid that she'd let the fear push her close to that extreme. She had managed the entire last year with Trevor stalking her across the country without a protector. But Duncan made her want to lean.

After carting her purchases in, she got herself ready for the shower. It would be a good distraction. It would keep her from obsessing over the incident this morning. She was dressed in one of two nice blouses she owned, her newest pair of jeans, and a pair of flats she had picked up.

She missed her knee-high black winter boots that she used to wear in Georgia this time of the year—not because Georgia received a lot of snow, but because it was a fashion statement.

It made her wonder what had happened to the house and all her family's possessions in the year she had been gone. Who was running the bank since she'd vanished? Had the city sold the house that had been in her family for three generations in her absence? Unless Trevor dropped dead, she would likely never know the answers to those questions.

Grabbing the black and white cookies she had baked the previous evening to keep herself busy while she was missing Duncan, she remembered to scoop up the gift, and headed out.

The exterior of Amber's home was impressive. It had a log cabin feel to it, but that was where any resemblance to the cabins on the property ended. It was a showplace— two stories tall, and it had to be a good four thousand square feet.

She pulled into the drive behind another truck. She climbed out of her vehicle as the woman from the red truck in front of hers stepped out. She was stunning, with long chestnut hair trailing down her back.

Eve pasted a smile on her face as she approached.

"Hey, you must be Eve. I'm Morgan Reed." She held out her hand with a cheery smile.

"Yes, I am. It's nice to meet you." Eve noticed the wedding band on Morgan's finger.

"I'm glad I'm not the only one who brought snacks." Morgan held up a tray.

"Can't help it. I was raised in the south, where if you

show up to a party without food, it brings shame on the whole family." Eve shrugged good naturedly.

"Ha! I like that. Me, I just have this problem where I like to cook all the time. Even with the mountain of food my boys go through in a sitting, I still manage to make too much."

"How many boys do you have?" Eve asked as they climbed the front porch stairs.

"Two, who love nothing more than giving me a run for my money."

"How old are they?"

"The twins will be five in February. And I'm trying to instill a little decency in them before sending them off to kindergarten."

"You don't look old enough to have a pair of five-year-olds."

"Oh, I'm their stepmama. Granted, I love those two knuckleheads as if they were my own."

"Does their mom help with raising them at all?" Eve was curious because Morgan still didn't look old enough to be running herd on a pair of twin boys.

"No. Unfortunately, their mom died when the boys were barely a year old. But I'm sure if she was alive, she would."

The door opened to reveal Amber, looking spectacular as always. Eve had never met a woman so expertly and smartly put together before. Even in jeans and a fancy soft red cashmere sweater, with a pair of heeled black boots, she looked phenomenal.

Amber grinned. "Morgan, Eve, so glad you two could

make it. Oh, and you both brought stuff to eat. That was so thoughtful. Come on in out of the cold."

They entered, and Amber took their coats. She glanced around the house. There was a formal living room, with a fire going in the fireplace. Christmas decorations covered every spare inch of space.

Amber walked them back to the family room. "Morgan, you already know everyone. Eve, you remember Grace, our mommy to be? Beside her is Bianca—she's engaged to Maverick, our head wrangler, they're going to be married this spring on the ranch. It's sure to be a festive occasion. Mrs. Gregory, our awesome cook and purveyor of the feast. And my bestest friend in the whole world, Noelle. We were roommates in college, and I convinced her—"

"You mean badgered, don't you?" Noelle interjected sarcastically with a droll glance, the movement shifting her dark auburn curls.

"All right, badgered into taking a teaching position at the local elementary and moving to Winter Park," Amber explained. "Everyone, this is Eve. She works at the hotel and is new to town."

"It's nice to see you again. And oh, you didn't have to bring me a gift," Grace said when she spied the bag in Eve's hands.

"It was my pleasure." She handed Grace the gift bag.

"And she brought cookies," Amber stated, taking the plate from Eve's hands and putting it on the table.

"Black and white cookies? Oh my god, gimme," Bianca exclaimed with a cultured British accent, reaching for the treats.

"You'll spoil your appetite for lunch," Mrs. Gregory stated.

"Oh, who cares? Not that I don't love your cooking, but I plan to eat all afternoon. And I promised to bring leftovers home for Maverick, since I'm not the best cook in the world," Bianca said.

"I've never had a black and white cookie. Are they good?" Grace asked, eyeing them with interest.

"Oh my god, yes. You've got to try them," Bianca stated, handing Grace one.

"And we've got chocolate chip cookies that Morgan made for our little gathering," Amber said, taking the tray from Morgan.

"I don't know how you do that with those two boys." Noelle shook her head.

"This coming from the second-grade teacher. How many seven-year-olds do you corral each day?" Morgan teased as she took one of the empty seats.

"They are only my legal responsibility between the hours of seven a.m. and three p.m. Monday through Friday. After that, they belong to their parents." Noelle bit into a chocolate chip cookie.

"Do you not like children?" Eve blurted out the question before she could think to stop herself.

Noelle laughed. "No, I happen to love them. Nothing gives me more joy than watching a little person learn and grow. That doesn't mean that I'm not realistic and aware enough to know how much of a handful they can be."

"Oh, don't tell me that. Not with D-Day approaching fast and furious," Grace bemoaned, rubbing her protruding baby bump.

"You'll be an excellent mother, Grace. That doesn't mean you won't have days when you want to pull your hair out, because you will," Mrs. Gregory explained with a wise intelligence in her gaze, like she had seen and done it all.

"Now that everyone is here, I thought we could have a toast. I even have sparkling grape juice for the mom to be." Amber held the two bottles in her hands.

"Better make that two on the sparkling juice." Morgan grinned slyly.

Amber, Bianca, and Grace gasped. Mrs. Gregory nodded her head like she approved. Noelle shook her head, and clapped.

"You're pregnant?" Grace asked.

"Yep." Morgan nodded with joy practically beaming from her body.

"That was fast," Bianca stated with a sigh.

"You should come in to the clinic. That way, we can get an ultrasound set up and—"

"I will. We weren't even sure we were going to start telling anyone but since there's alcohol today, I figured I'd better. But please don't say anything to my boys. We're telling them Christmas morning. They've been pestering the daylights out of us to give them a sister," Morgan explained.

"You do realize you've screwed me, right? First Grace, and now you. Maverick is going to start talking about babies again. Problem is that I love that man to distraction, and will likely cave." Bianca shook her head with exasperation.

"Do you not want kids?" Noelle asked.

"No, I do, very much so, but I would also like to fit into my wedding dress in four months. After that, well, like I said, that man could convince me to do almost anything." Bianca sighed with a small smile playing around her lips and a look in her eyes that made Eve feel jealous. It was the look of a woman who knew in no uncertain terms that she was loved.

Amber handed out the champagne glasses, giving the two expectant mothers ones filled with juice. Then she held her glass in the air. "To Grace, on the advent of welcoming her little boy. And to Morgan, you're braver than all of us combined to welcome another addition, and we are so happy for you both. Cheers!"

"Cheers."

"Congrats."

"Now, who's hungry? Mrs. Gregory helped make this lovely spread." Amber gestured to the side table that was nigh buckling beneath the weight of the food on top.

They sat around the family room, eating and chatting. It had been so long since Eve had had a group of female friends to talk to, it was almost novel. She laughed. She found herself discussing the merits of bottle feeding versus breast feeding. She and Morgan really seemed to click—even though she was a few years younger—discussing some of their favorite baking recipes and gadgets.

When they had all finished lunch, Mrs. Gregory rose from her seat. "Thank you for having me, but this old woman needs a nap before I start working on the hotel menu for the next few weeks."

"Are you sure?" Amber asked her, concern dotting her brow.

"Yes, I'm fine. Wipe that look off your face, missy. I may be old but I'm in no way ready to meet my maker," Mrs. Gregory stated. "Grace, have that man of yours call me if there's anything you need. I'll make sure the two of you are fed when the little one arrives, so there's nothing for you to worry about there."

Grace tried to rise from her seat.

Mrs. Gregory walked over to her and gave her a hug. "You get some rest now, too, ya hear?"

"I will. Thank you for coming, and for the amazing lunch." Grace hugged her back.

"It was my pleasure, dear. No, don't get up. I can see myself out." Mrs. Gregory waved them all off.

They heard Mrs. Gregory speaking to someone at the front door before she left. Heavy booted footsteps thudded over the hardwood. Lincoln, the cowboy who had followed Eve's truck a while back, entered the family room with his hat in his hands.

He stared at Amber. "Sorry to barge in like this, Amber. If I could talk to you for a minute? We've got an issue with one of the guest cabins."

"Um, sure. If you're hungry, we've got plenty of food." Amber gestured to the buffet.

"I can see that. Ladies, sorry for interrupting your feminine ritual. I'll be out of your hair in two shakes." Lincoln nodded at them.

"Follow me," Amber said, breezing by him without a glance.

Lincoln followed her path with his eyes first—they

were stark with hunger—before he seemed to remember he had an audience. He nodded at the group, then followed Amber.

Their muted conversation trickled down the hall. But it was Bianca who broke the stillness. "So, a little birdie told me that you're dating Duncan?"

"Wait, what? I hadn't heard that. Is that true?" Morgan asked, her mouth open in surprise.

"Yes. I guess we are. I mean, the only reason he's not at my place and I'm not at his is because he's leading a camping trip this weekend," Eve admitted with a small shrug.

Grace chuckled. "You lucky girl. Duncan's a good guy."

"Am I the only single one here?" Noelle said, grabbing a cookie off the table.

"Nope. You're not the only one." Amber waltzed back into the room with a sigh, went straight to the bottle of champagne, and topped her glass off.

"Girl, you've got to stop mooning over that one," Bianca said, holding her champagne glass out for a refill.

"Especially if you're not going to do anything about it," Grace added, shooting Amber a knowing look.

"Why haven't you done anything about it?" Eve asked, rather curious at seeing a new side to her boss.

Amber rolled her shoulders and sighed. "We rub each other the wrong way. Making me a complete mental case for wanting to climb that man like a tree, but there you have it."

"What about Matt or Eli? They're both gorgeous, and would likely leave you feeling great instead of miserable,"

Noelle stated, like she was surprised Amber hadn't thought of that before now.

"It's hard wanting someone you think you can't have," Eve added. "But after watching Lincoln, I've got to say I think that guy has the hots for you."

Amber gave her a lopsided grin. "You think? Between you and Duncan, who caved first?"

"I really do. Lincoln looked at you when you walked down that hall, like you were what he wanted to take a bite out of, not the finger sandwiches. And I was the one who suggested we get horizontal together that first time."

"There, you see? I've been telling you Amber, if you want Lincoln, do something about it. You need to make the first move," Bianca said, toasting her champagne glass in Eve's direction.

Amber sighed. "He's my employee, which makes the situation a little bit more complicated than that. But I will think on it. You were saying, Eve?"

"Oh nothing, my making the first move was as much of a surprise to me as it was to Duncan, mainly because I haven't dated in forever," Eve explained without really thinking about what she was saying.

"With your looks? Why the hell not?" Bianca asked with her brows raised.

"It's complicated." More than just a little bit.

"You can tell us. We're all friends here. Whatever you're comfortable with," Amber said with such genuine warmth that Eve was touched by it.

And for the first time in forever, she felt like unloading the weight of her problems. She had already been debating about opening up to them. Maybe they would be a good test run, and help her figure out how to tell Duncan.

Screwing up her courage, she explained, "I've had to move around a lot over the past year. It hasn't left time for dating." Or feeling safe and secure, or feeling like she could trust someone and not get them killed.

"Why all the moving? In trouble with the law or something?" Morgan asked with a little laugh.

"Morgan!" Amber exclaimed.

"It's okay if you don't want to tell us. But we're here if you need someone to talk to about it," Grace said, the calm voice of reason.

Eve swallowed. "It's okay. I need to get it off my chest, and figure out a way to explain it to Duncan. The thing is... five years ago, I was in a hostage situation at a bank. I saw both men's faces who perpetrated the armed robbery. I paid attention throughout the whole ordeal. It was my testimony that helped put the men in prison. One of them died in prison two years ago, but the other was released on parole a year ago. They were brothers, you see. And he's... well, suffice to say, he holds me responsible for his brother's death, and came after me."

"Oh god, honey." Amber put her hand over hers.

"I can't believe you've been through all that," Bianca stated with a hand on her chest.

"That's insane." Morgan shook her head.

"Has he hurt you?" Noelle asked, looking at Eve with a patient expression she likely used with her second graders.

"Yes. I've been on the run ever since," Eve admitted, feeling like a weight was being lifted off her shoulders.

She hadn't realized how much she'd needed to tell someone.

"How can we help?" Grace asked.

"And you haven't told Duncan?" Amber questioned with her head tilted.

"To hell with Duncan, do the police know?" Bianca demanded with a furious scowl.

"I haven't told him yet. Honestly, I've been a little worried about how he will react." Because then she might have to tell him that Eve wasn't her real name. And that if her real name was used anywhere, Trevor would find her. She knew he would. "And the police won't do anything unless he tries to harm me. They can't arrest him without any evidence of wrong doing. I filed a restraining order, but a piece of paper won't keep someone with a vendetta away."

"Do you think he knows where you are now?" Amber asked, her expression thoughtful.

Eve shook her head. "No. I don't. If he did, he would be here already." But oh God, she hoped that he hadn't found her yet. Even after her scare earlier today, she was holding on to hope that this time would be different.

"I'm glad you told us. But I think you should tell Duncan, too, as soon as possible," Amber stated with a kind understanding in her eyes.

"Yeah, men are funny where their women are concerned—and protecting them. He'll be more pissed if you wait to tell him," Grace murmured thoughtfully.

"Aren't they though?" Bianca nodded in agreement.

"I know if I held something like this back from Noah, he would be mighty pissed off with me," Morgan stated.

"I will. As soon as he gets back from his camping trip tomorrow," Eve said.

"Good." Amber nodded her approval. "Now, who's ready for some games?"

Eve would do it, too: tell Duncan about Trevor. At least she'd give him more than what she had on their camping trip, because if she gave him these morsels to chew on, he would stop digging. Then she had a real chance of a life here—with him.

21

*R*ather tired from his camping trip, after his shower, Duncan started a load of laundry. He'd have to figure out something for dinner tonight since it didn't look like Mrs. Gregory had had the chance to cook him something.

But then he thought maybe he should give Eve a call. See if she would like to go out for dinner. It was something they had yet to do, which was odd, especially considering they had been together every night the past week.

His desire for her seemed to be growing and not diminishing. The more he had her, the more he wanted her. She hadn't asked him for commitment, which was unexpected. And in some ways, it made her unique as well. She was different than other women he had encountered. She seemed surprised that he wanted to spend time with her. And when it came to commitment, he was considering asking her for it.

It was something he hadn't done with a woman in

years. But after the night at Cabin X, where she had opened beautifully for him, he wondered if she would be able to withstand some of his darker elements. If he was a betting man, from what he had seen of her so far, he thought that she would. And the thought was intoxicating, giving him all sorts of ideas, like collaring her, permanence, and even the institute of marriage, which for him was a big motherfucking deal. He didn't take commitment at that level lightly.

Because there was something about her, like tumblers of a lock slipping into place inside him.

At the knock on the front door, Sampson rose from his spot on the floor in front of the fireplace and ambled over, his tail wagging. Duncan followed the pup and felt a kick in the gut at spying Eve on his doorstep, holding a casserole dish and with a reusable grocery bag slung over a slim shoulder.

"Hi, I know you just got back. But I figured you'd be tired. I made this for you and—"

"That was sweet of you. Come in. Have dinner with me." He ushered her inside. The moment the food was on the counter, he tugged her into his arms and kissed her, needing the taste of her on his tongue after two nights without her. She didn't deny him. He pressed his advantage until the moment he felt her go pliant against him.

He lifted his mouth, running his hands over her back. "Hi. Miss me?"

"And if I did?"

"Then I would say you weren't the only one. I like having you here, Eve, both in my bed and out of it."

Surprised pleasure spread over her features. "I like it too."

"I'll get some plates out." He kissed her on the forehead before releasing her.

"It needs a few minutes heating up in the oven. I've got salad. And I'll need a cookie sheet to heat up the garlic bread," she said, pulling items out of the bag and putting them on the counter.

"I can get that for you. Would you like a beer? Sorry, I'm all out of wine because someone drank it all," he teased, rather pleased by her blushing and just how right she looked in his house.

"Beer would be great. So how was your weekend?"

"It went fine. Two brothers with their sons wanting to teach them all about camping and outdoor survival. They had a good time."

"That's nice. It's good that you enjoy your job as much as you do."

"Do you not like working for the ranch?"

"The ranch, yes, the job itself, not so much. But I think it ends up being a wash for me. I spent yesterday with Amber, Grace, Bianca, Morgan, and Noelle at Grace's baby shower. It's nice having female friends again. I feel like this is a place that could be home for me."

"Do you now?" That was good. If she was planning on being here for the long haul, then there was a chance they could make a go of this relationship.

They spent the next few minutes setting the table. She dished up the lasagna and salad, putting the garlic bread on a plate between them.

"It looks great, honey. I missed your cooking."

"Save some room. There's apple pie for dessert."

"Oh, man." He groaned around a bite. He should propose just to make sure she kept cooking for him.

Where the hell had that thought come from? Propose? But as the idea lingered and settled, it started feeling right instead of terrifying.

"How was the baby shower?" he asked.

"Good. Morgan's pregnant."

"Is she now? Noah moved fast on that one, not that I blame him. They're perfect for each other." The errant thought rose up in his mind, wondering what he would feel if Eve got pregnant. Even though she was on birth control, accidents did happen. And since they weren't using condoms any longer, it left the possibility there, however slight it might be that she could wind up carrying his kid.

"Yeah. They aren't telling the boys yet. Not until Christmas morning, as one of their gifts, so this information needs to stay between you and me."

He laughed. "Those two are trouble with a capital T. Pair of hellions bent on destruction."

"They can't be that bad. They're only four."

"They're worse. Although, I must admit, since Morgan came into the picture and became their step-mama, they've definitely improved. Anything else happen while I was away?"

She straightened in her chair and fidgeted with the beer bottle. "I know you've been curious about why I want to learn self-defense. I told you on the camping trip that someone I trusted hurt me. And I know that you've asked about what happened."

"Eve, when you're ready to tell, you'll tell me." He took a swig of beer, hoping that he had finally earned her trust enough for her to tell him her story.

"That's what I'm trying to say, that I'm ready. And I know you may not like it all, but—"

Finally! Thank fuck! It warmed him deep into the recesses of his soul that she was finally able to trust him enough with the demons that were hounding her. "Take a deep breath. Tell me whatever you feel comfortable with. You know that you can trust me. Right?"

"Yes. Absolutely."

"Good. I'm listening." He went back to eating his meal, hoping to alleviate some of the tension rolling off her now. But he no longer tasted the amazing food. His focus shifted to Eve, and listening to her.

"See, the deal is, five years ago, I was in a hostage situation at a bank. I saw the men's faces. One of them was the guy I was seeing at the time. The other thief was his brother. While they were robbing the bank, I paid attention throughout the whole ordeal—mainly because I was so stunned that it was the two of them."

Holy shit! It was way worse than he had imagined, and he had imagined plenty.

She took a drink before continuing. "And because I paid attention, it was my testimony that helped put them in jail. The man I had been dating, who used me to get information on the bank, died in prison two years ago. His brother was released on parole a little over a year ago. And he holds me responsible for his brother's death."

Everything inside Duncan hardened. He had to force his fingers to relax around the fork in his hand instead of mangling it into an unrecognizable shape in his anger. It all made sense now. She made sense. The way she had acted like a scared rabbit when she first arrived at the ranch. Even the way she fought her attraction, stopping him before it proceeded past a hot kiss. But he had to know. "And he's after you?"

Fear flashed in her eyes. It made Duncan want to scoop her up, do whatever he needed to do to keep her safe. No one was harming a hair on her head on his watch. He would guard her until his dying breath.

She nodded. "He was, and might still be. I've moved around a lot over the past year. The police won't do anything about it. I tried them first, shortly after he was released from prison."

"Has he found you?" Duncan asked, ready to do violence upon the man for even thinking about her.

She flinched at the menace in his voice. "A couple of times. I spent a month riding buses around the country before I came here. Zigzagging, paying cash for everything, and think I finally lost him."

It was doubtful. It depended on the guy's background. If he and his brother used her as a mark to set up an armed robbery, he was a professional criminal. They didn't back down when they were carrying out vendettas. They had the tools, resources, money, and network at their disposal. "What's his name?"

"That's not important." She wouldn't meet Duncan's eyes. She sat at the table, twisting her hands together.

"Name. Now," he demanded.

Her head shot up at his dominant tone. In her eyes were layers of fear. He hated that she had been through so much—and on her own, it appeared. But he spied courage also as she straightened in her seat. "Trevor Cleveland."

Duncan nodded. He would notify the local sheriff, have him look this Trevor dude up. Then he would get his picture and make sure every man on the ranch knew to be on the lookout for the son of a bitch. No one would harm Eve. He wouldn't allow it.

Duncan rose from his seat and rounded the table.

"Thank you for telling me. Now..." he lifted her out of her chair, feeling the tension slide out of her as he carried her to the bedroom, "want to get naked?"

"I thought you'd never ask." The smile on her face sucker punched him, and he felt his heart drop into his toes.

Because he realized this wasn't just a passing fling for him. He was in love with Eve.

---

22

*F*ive days before Christmas, a doozy of a snowstorm hit the ranch. Outside the hotel, it was near whiteout conditions. Eve was working to clean the first floor as they set up tables in the lobby for all the guests and workers stranded by the storm.

Amber stood, much like a general on the battlefield, issuing orders to the staff. But she was one of the generals who didn't mind getting her hands dirty. She had rolled up her sleeves and was working with Mike from registration and Mrs. Gregory to arrange a hot beverage station, a soup and chili station, sandwiches, and more.

The hotel door by the reception desk opened, bringing with it a billowing plume of snow and icy winds. A man emerged carrying something heavy in his arms. It took Eve a moment to realize it was a someone and not a something. It was Grace, bundled from head to toe, her face contorted with pain.

"Emmett?" Amber exclaimed with panic lacing her voice as she approached the couple. "What's going on?"

"Grace is in labor. The storm is so fucking bad I can't see shit to drive us to the hospital. We need to hole up here until it passes. And anyone planning on leaving the hotel, you need to tell them to stay. It's really bad out there."

"Everything is going to be just fine. Jessica, I need a room I can put them in. Mike, contact Matt. He's helping Maverick with the cattle. Tell him Grace is in labor. He was a medic in the military, and should be able to help. Mrs. Gregory, I'm leaving you in charge of the food," Amber stated. "Eve, why don't you come with us and help me get Grace situated."

If Eve was ever in a tight spot, she wanted Amber there to handle things. The woman didn't waver or flinch. She did what was necessary, with the least amount of fuss.

"I'm right behind you." Eve set the mop and bucket out of the way. There was no way to keep the first floor clean with this much billowing snow encroaching inside every time the door was opened, anyway.

They took Grace to the presidential suite. In the room, Amber said, "Go grab the shower curtain, we're going to lay it underneath Grace. Do that while I pull out the sofa bed. This way, the main bed will be available once Grace has delivered."

Eve nodded, working on autopilot as Amber directed her. In the bathroom, she texted Duncan.

Stuck at the hotel. Grace is here, and in labor. I'm helping. Probably going to be snowed in here. Be safe.

Pocketing the cell, she pulled the shower curtain down. But before she walked back into the living room, her phone buzzed in her pocket. She glanced at it quickly.

Sampson and I will meet you there once we're done. Is there anything Grace and Emmett need?

She headed into the living room and said to Emmett, "Duncan needs to know if you need anything?"

"I left the overnight bag with extra clothes for Grace, clothes and diapers for the baby in the back seat. And Grace's medical bag that we will likely need is right beside it. The truck is open."

"I'll tell him."

Emmett said both Grace's medical bag and overnight bag with Grace and baby's stuff they will need are in the backseat of his truck parked outside the hotel. Truck is open.

I'll get them. Should be done in the next hour. Tell them Matt is on the way, he replied.

Will do.

She pocketed her phone. "Matt's on his way."

"Thank god," Emmett said, helping Grace out of her coat.

Eve and Amber made up the sofa bed with the protective layer beneath the sheets. "I feel like we should be boiling water. Don't they always boil water in these types of situations?" she asked.

Amber chuckled. "You're probably not far off."

"Towels. I have the sterile equipment in my medical bag. Ice chips for me, since this could take a while. Whiskey for Emmett so he doesn't lose his mind. And... oh, sweet Jesus." Grace's face scrunched up. Her knees buckled from the pain, and there was a sound of gushing water.

Emmett caught her before she slid to the ground. "Come on, Doc, you've got this. Deep breaths for me, love."

"Emmett, why don't we get Grace cleaned up in the bathroom and then into bed where she will be more comfortable. Eve—"

"I'm on it. I've got this. You help Grace."

Eve spent the next fifteen minutes cleaning the hardwood floor. She had never realized there was so much when a woman's water broke. Once it was all mopped up and she had sterilized the floor, she left the room and headed to the supply closet at the end of the hall. Grace had said they were going to need towels, so she grabbed a huge stack of them.

Loading her arms up, she headed back to the suite.

Amber and Emmett were settling Grace on the sofa bed as Eve waltzed in with the stack of towels.

"If this isn't enough, I can get more." She deposited them next to the television.

"Thanks for grabbing those."

There was a knock on the door. Since Eve was closest, she headed over and opened the door.

"Hey, I hear someone is in labor and needs my skills. I'm Matt." He held out his hand for her to shake. He had a rakish charm that was rather engaging and sweet.

"Eve. Come on in." She stepped back, giving him room to enter.

Matt swaggered in and headed straight over to Grace.

"Well, now. I see you've got to do things the hard way, huh?"

Grace laughed and then scowled. "Dammit, don't do that, make me laugh. It hurts too damn much."

"Let me go wash my hands. And then I'm going to need to take a look at your progress," Matt explained, putting his hat beside the stack of towels.

"Bet you didn't think this was how your day was going to go, huh?" Grace joked.

"It's better than being out in that white shit. And frankly, better than anything I had to deal with in a field tent in Afghanistan. Emmett, why don't you get her back propped up a bit while I'm washing my hands?" Matt ordered before he strode out of the room and headed into the bathroom.

Emmett helped Grace breathe through another contraction, then shifted her slightly on the bed like Matt had instructed. The love between Grace and Emmett was palpable. It made Eve ache over their bond.

She watched as Matt returned, got down, and examined Grace. "You're looking good. But I would say that you're only at about three centimeters. So, we have a ways to go before we can deliver."

"The baby is early. Three weeks. We just did an ultra-sound last week and the doctor said he was fully developed," Emmett said while his wife panted through another contraction, gripping her husband's hand hard enough, her knuckles turned white.

"That's good. I'm trained in emergency medicine. I just need to get some supplies to cut the umbilical cord, and do stitches if they are needed." Matt seemed to be assessing the situation with calmness.

"In my medical bag... in the truck... even have tiny fetal heart monitor," Grace gasped and panted through the pain.

"I can go get it. It's parked right outside?" Matt asked, rising from his spot on the sofa bed.

"There's no need." Duncan strode in, carrying both bags, with Sampson hot on his heels.

"Thanks, Duncan. Why don't you and Eve head down to registration. Help Jessica and Mike get people into rooms for the night—and that includes you both," Amber stated, assuming command once more.

"We can do that. Congrats, you two. If you need us for anything, just call," Duncan said, and steered Eve from the room.

"How is it outside?"

He ushered her onto the elevator. "One of the worst storms I've seen in years, and it doesn't seem to be letting up. But at least we're stuck at the hotel. They've got plenty of solar powered generators that are always fully charged. So, we don't need to worry about losing power or heat. There's plenty of food and water."

"And if there's an issue with the baby or Grace?" Eve asked, finally voicing the concern.

"We'll figure it out if that's the case. In the meantime, we pray that everything comes out fine," he said as the doors opened on the first floor.

She and Duncan helped get the stranded employees at the hotel set up in available rooms. Duncan put the two of them together in a room.

Eve helped Mrs. Gregory for a time with serving up chili and soup, and replenishing the coffee, hot tea, and hot cocoa. Some of the cowboys taking care of the animals came in from time to time to warm up with a hot cup of coffee and a meal.

The horses and cattle had all been safely retrieved from the fields. The horses were bedded down with extra hay in the stables. The cattle had been rounded up and were riding the storm out in the barns. The cowboys were taking shifts with the animals.

Periodically, Eve headed up to the room with more ice chips, checking on the birth progress. Later that evening, she and Duncan were eating some soup and sandwiches for dinner in the lobby when Matt sauntered in looking haggard, like he had run his hands through his hair a million times that day, but with a smile on his face that was endearing.

Duncan waved him over. "Any news?"

"Emmett and Grace have a beautiful, healthy baby boy. Mom and baby are doing great." Matt smiled with exhaustion.

"I should take them some dinner." Eve rose from her seat, needing something to do.

"I can help you," Duncan offered.

"They might not want a parade yet," Eve said.

"They were fairly exhausted but checking the little one out," Matt added.

"See? I'll be back quickly." She gave Duncan a quick kiss, much to Matt's amusement, then headed over to the tables with the food. She grabbed a tray and filled it with some sandwiches, soup, tea and cocoa. She remembered to grab some utensils and napkins, put the tray on a rolling cart that room service used to deliver meals to guests, then wheeled the cart to the suite.

She knocked on the door. Amber answered. "Eve, oh, that's so sweet of you. I was just thinking of getting them a bite. Come on in."

"Matt told us the good news. I figured they had to be hungry."

"Starving," Grace murmured as Eve entered with the rolling tray.

They had moved the family into the main king bed. Grace was resting against a mound of pillows with a small bundle in her arms. Beside her, with his arm around Grace's shoulders, was Emmett. And in all her life, Eve had never seen a man so happy.

She wheeled the cart over to the bedside. "I've got soup, sandwiches, chips, cookies, hot tea, hot cocoa, and lemonade."

"That was so thoughtful of you, Eve, thanks for bringing it. And we would like to introduce you to Jameson Michael Benson. Little Jamie certainly made an entrance, much like his father." Grace held her little bundle up so Eve could see the sweet, sleeping face.

Emmett chuckled. "You wouldn't have it any other way."

Grace blushed and glanced at her husband. There was such love between them. "I'm sure our son is going to raise just as much hell as his daddy."

"I'll teach him all my tricks."

"He's beautiful. I'll get out of your hair. I'm sure you

guys are exhausted," Eve said, thinking she didn't want to intrude further on the new family.

Emmett scratched his head. "I should check on the horses. See if Mav needs any—"

"Don't even think about it, Emmett. We've got the animals covered. You're officially on family leave for the next month. And don't even try to wiggle out of it," Amber stated with her hands on her hips.

"But I—"

Amber pointed at him. "No. You stay here with Grace until the snow stops and roads are clear enough that we can get Grace and Jamie to the hospital to have them checked out. Other than that, rest, take care of Grace and Jamie."

"Babe, I think you'd better listen to her," Grace murmured with a yawn.

Emmett glanced at his son and then his wife. "Fine. Jamie, what do you say you and I let your mama eat?"

Before Eve left, she watched Grace transfer Jamie into Emmett's strong arms. Little Jamie waved his hands in the air, like he was excited at the prospect of hanging with his daddy.

"Thanks for bringing food, Eve. You're a lifesaver," Grace stated, eyeing the tray.

"It's no problem. Congrats again, you guys." Eve headed out the door to look for Duncan, but he was already there.

"Hey, do you want to meet their son? He's beautiful."

"I figure they'll want some family time. Tomorrow will be soon enough. I'm here to take you to bed."

Duncan gripped her arm and steered her toward the elevator. Sampson padded beside them.

She sighed. "It has been one hell of a long day. But I'm glad you're here with me, and not stuck at your cabin."

"I am, too." He pulled her into the elevator. They were the only ones on board when he continued, "Because I plan to strip you down and make you scream with pleasure."

"But what about our neighbors? The hotel is full."

"Let them hear, and be jealous," he teased seductively.

In their room, Sampson curled up on the couch but Eve's focus shifted to the man undressing before her. He was beautiful, in that rugged male way of his, and all hers. She loved him. And, deep in her heart, she wished that he would love her back.

They tumbled into bed, their hands roving and caressing hungrily like it had been weeks since they had touched instead of hours. She infused her touch with the love she felt, hoping to impart it a little bit and let him feel it, since she was too afraid to voice those feelings.

What started as a hot, hungry race to the finish line shifted into passionate, intense lovemaking. When Duncan slid inside, his movements slowed. Clasping their hands together as they moved together in a sinuous dance as old as time, while the storm raged outside, another one thundered between them.

She clung to him, her arms around his back as they rocked together, driving toward a pinnacle so beautiful and earth shattering, tears fell from her eyes as she climaxed, and felt him follow her over.

Later, with his arm around her, his big body shielding her back, she slipped into a dreamless sleep, feeling safe and cherished.

hristmas Eve dawned with golden sunshine. Eve was coming to believe she had a place here at Silver Springs Ranch. That this place was the fresh start she needed. She had a job she was finally settling into, a man she had fallen head over heels for, who was brimming with potential for the future, and people she was coming to care about.

The truth was, she could see herself living here long term, eventually moving in with Duncan as their relationship deepened. She wanted to commit herself to him, body and soul. And she was even coming to believe that she could tell him her real name. He had taken the story about Trevor and her moving around the country in stride—better than she had imagined he would.

She was thoroughly enjoying spending her nights with his arms around her and then waking in the weak hours of the morning, feeling him sliding deep inside her before she was fully awake. Just like he had this morning before he had headed off to work—in the stables, since they weren't doing any camping trips for the time being.

They were eking out their foundation little by little. And she wanted to continue building it with him.

She had left his cabin with Sampson in tow. Duncan didn't take him to the stables because the goofy dog would roll in the horse manure. Duncan had asked her to keep him close. It was his way of trying to protect her when he wasn't around, and Eve thought it was sweet.

She was off for the next few days, for the holidays. She had spent the morning cooking and baking dishes to bring to the new parents. Given the temperatures were in the teens and would be dropping into single digits by nightfall, she dressed warmly, layering thermal bottoms and a long sleeved top over her bra and panties before donning her jeans and mauve flannel top.

As she dressed, she couldn't help but think about the way Duncan had left this morning.

She had been sipping coffee and stowing dirty dishes in the dishwasher after their breakfast. He came up behind her and slid his arms around her waist. "Any plans for Christmas day?"

"No. You?"

"I was thinking that you should pack a bag and stay with me tonight."

"You want to spend Christmas with me?" she had asked breathlessly.

"Mmmhmm. I figure we could spend the day in bed."

"As long as you promise to get up and open your present at some point, I'm game."

"You got me a gift?" he asked with pleased surprise lacing his voice.

"I did. It's small. You don't have to—"

His lips closed over hers, and he just about devoured her with that kiss.

She sighed at the memory. It was what she wanted, to build more memories with him.

Checking the time, she put the meals in a box she had grabbed at the grocery store the other day to make it easier to cart the stuff over to Grace and Emmett's cabin. She loaded all the food up in the back seat and on the floorboard. Sampson liked to sit shotgun so he could look out the window.

She had to admit, the sweet pup with his penchant for mischief had come to mean the world to her too. He was a great cuddler. At night, when she and Duncan sat on the couch to watch a movie together, she would curl up beside Duncan, usually with her head on his shoulder. Sampson always joined them up on the couch, and would lay his head across her lap.

It was just so homey.

Once she had everything in the truck, she grabbed Sampson, and they were off. The drive to Grace and Emmett's place didn't take all that long. But then, the ranch was its own contained universe—one of the things she liked about it the most.

Amber answered the door. Sampson made a beeline inside before she could stop him.

"Sampson, dammit."

"Oh, he's fine," Eve heard Grace's voice say.

"Do you need a hand?" Amber asked.

"If you would take these, I have one more box in the car."

"Sure thing." Amber took the box inside for her while Eve trudged back to the truck. She grabbed the box full of pastries, then headed in.

"What's all this?" Grace asked, holding her son.

Morgan and Bianca were laughing over the two boys who were wrestling with Sampson on the floor. Eve didn't see Noelle but wondered if she still had school. She wasn't sure when the elementary school started their Christmas holiday break. Although, considering it was Christmas Eve, it was sure to start soon.

"I figured you and Emmett will likely be so busy with the newest addition, I thought I would bring some easy meals for you guys to heat up."

"Oh, that was so thoughtful of you," Grace said, and got a little teary eyed. "Sorry, hormones."

"It's nothing fancy, just a few hearty casserole dishes. Christmas cookies, scones, and fresh bread."

"You bake bread?" Morgan asked, joining them in the kitchen.

"Yes, baking calms me. I like doing it all from scratch."

"I still haven't perfected bread making. Maybe we should have a day where we swap recipes," Morgan offered.

"That sounds fun." It warmed Eve's heart how accepting these ladies had been with her. They had taken her in and made her one of them without question.

"What other things can you bake?" Bianca asked, snagging one of the Christmas cookies.

"Chess squares, any type of cookie really, cakes, pies, puff pastries. Really anything. I've even branched out and learned a few recipes with almond and coconut flour for people who have a gluten issue."

"Have you ever considered opening your own bakery?" Morgan asked with an interested gleam in her eyes.

"I did, for a while."

"Why didn't you pursue it?" Amber asked, biting into a Christmas cookie.

"My parents died. I was left to take over the family business and it didn't leave time for something like that." Then she wanted to kick herself for revealing that much.

"You and I should talk, Eve. Not to take you away from the ranch, so please don't hurt me, Amber, but I've been thinking about starting a bakery in town. There's this great little shop that's available. I've already looked at what it would cost to get the right ovens installed and get it up to code. And... oh, listen to me. I could go on. And I know it's insane, given I'm pregnant and am going to have my hands full, but if I had a partner..." Morgan dangled the thread as she trailed off.

"I can see I'm going to have to move up my plans. Before the two of you decide on that, I wanted to offer you space for your own bakery in the main hotel, Eve. If you and Morgan wanted to be partners on it, that is definitely something we can discuss. It would be your bakery, but I would have a stake in it as one of the partners. And as one of the partners, you would get the space for free. I can invest some overhead to help get it off the ground, to come out of the profits over, say, three years, but then the profits would be split equally," Amber stated.

Morgan looked like she wanted to tap dance across the floor.

"But what about the maid position?" Eve asked, not really believing that life could be shaping up to be everything she'd ever wanted.

"Eve, you're a hard worker. I admire that about you. And you're a good maid. But you're an excellent baker. Not a single one of your creations has been bad. Not even those meringue cookies. I loathe meringue, but not when you make it," Amber stated with a shake of her head.

"Can I think about it?"

"Yes, but don't take too long. Because if Morgan is coming aboard, we've got, what, six-seven months before she's due? It means we'll have to work fast if we would want to launch by spring," Amber said with a calculated look.

"Where would we be working out of in the hotel? If you don't mind my asking," Morgan said, handing her boys each a cookie and giving them side eye. Basically, it was mom code for: *behave, or else.*

"There's room to expand at the back of the lobby. I've already discussed it with Lincoln. Where I'm thinking of adding on won't mess with the structural integrity of the hotel."

"Would we be able to carry box lunches too? For the people who don't want a sit-down meal but something fast and easy to carry?" Morgan asked.

Amber smiled. "You're speaking my language. Interested, Eve?"

Was she? Hell, yes. "I would be lying if I said that I wasn't. Perhaps the three of us should sit down after the holidays and discuss logistics, percentages, that kind of thing."

Morgan did a little fist pump and bootie wiggle. "This is going to be so much fun. I can't wait to tell Noah."

"Come on, let's sit in the living room and eat some of these fabulous cookies. Morgan, do you mind bringing them over?" Grace asked.

They all sat in the living room, laughing and sighing over the cuteness overload that was Jamie. He really was a sweet little thing, and so tiny. And for a moment, Eve wondered what a baby with Duncan would look like.

The front door slammed open.

They all jumped. Jamie issued a piercing cry at being startled. Cold blasted inside, and Eve shivered.

"Emmett, look what you did! Babe, you can't come slamming into..." Grace trailed off. Her face went sheet white. And she held Jamie even closer.

A chill danced along Eve's spine as she turned to face the door. The sight that greeted her sent her heart plummeting into the ground.

Trevor. Wearing a damn black patch over the eye she had injured more than a year ago.

He'd found her. Menace pumped off him in lacerating waves.

How stupid Eve had been to get involved with the people here. She had put everyone in danger. How quickly all the dreams she had begun spinning crashed and burned before they even had the chance to make it off the ground.

"Did you really think you had seen the last of me?" Trevor exclaimed, lifting a hand gun and waving it around the room.

Out of the corner of her eye, Eve spied Morgan with her arms wrapped protectively around the twins. Their frightened little faces broke her heart.

Sampson rose from his spot on the floor, growling. His lips curled with intimidation as he spied the danger that Trevor presented.

"Shut him up. I'll shoot him."

"Sampson. Down." Eve gave him the same command Duncan did. At the thought of Duncan, she bit her trembling lip.

Sampson obeyed with a whine, plopping his butt next to her on the floor. The boys started crying. She hated that they were so upset. It was all her fault.

"You're here for me." Eve rose from her seat and shook her head no at Amber, when she looked like she was going to stand up too.

"Don't harm them. I will come with you of my own free will, as long as you leave them alone."

"Why should I?" Trevor snarled.

"Because my death won't matter all that much, and you'll likely get away. But a house full of women and children? The cops will hunt you down to the ends of the earth, and you know it. Not even you can survive that."

Trevor glowered as he pointed the gun at her chest.

The strange thing was, Eve wasn't afraid for herself at all—which was likely stupid on her part, considering the gig was up and she didn't see a way out of this for herself. But she was terrified for her friends and their children. She wanted Sampson protected so that Duncan would have someone when she was gone.

Trevor seemed to be calculating her words. Then he waved her toward him with the gun. "Come. You want these bitches and their brats to live, you come with me right now."

She nodded. "I will."

"Eve," Amber protested.

Eve shot her a look and shook her head. "Tell Duncan, I'm sorry. Tell him..." she blinked back an onslaught of tears, "goodbye for me. Bianca, hold Sampson by his collar so he can't come after me."

"Two seconds before I change my mind," Trevor warned, his voice full of menace.

Eve sucked in a ragged breath. After a last glance at her friends' faces, she walked toward Trevor. "Can I get my coat?"

He snorted derisively. "Bitch, where you're going, you won't need it."

When she was close enough, he grabbed her with his free arm and dragged her toward the door. She didn't put up a fight. She had to get him away from them. And giving herself up like this was the only surefire way to protect them.

He didn't bother shutting the door. Sampson started whining. The twins' wails followed her outside.

Trevor dragged her over to a silver Chevy truck. At the passenger door, he waved the gun at her. "Get in."

When she didn't move fast enough for his liking, he

shoved her into the front passenger seat. Stowing the gun in his pants, he grabbed her wrists and bound them with a length of rope. Once she was secure, he slammed the door shut, marched around to the driver's side, and leapt in.

As he backed out, Eve spotted Amber standing at the open cabin doorway on the phone. It looked like she was relaying information to someone. But then Trevor sped away from the cabin.

Eve wondered if she would live to see nightfall, and just how much her death was going to hurt.

Her only regret in life was that she had never told Duncan that she loved him. And now it was too late.

24

*D*uncan was looking forward to the holiday—for the first time in years, if he was honest. In the Navy, he'd gotten used to not celebrating with family. Not that his family was big on the celebration, so it had ended up becoming just another day.

But he was looking forward to this one. And it was all because of Eve.

He finally understood why Colt had left everything behind to be with Avery. Because when a man found the right woman, it changed everything, and there was nothing he wouldn't do for her. Including saying a fond farewell to his bachelor status.

Little by little, some of her things had started showing up at his place—with his encouragement, of course. She had a spare toothbrush in the holder by the sink. Bottles of her shampoo and conditioner were in his shower.

He wondered what she would do when he asked her to move in with him tomorrow. It was a big step for him.

He'd never lived with a woman he wasn't related to, but then, he hadn't wanted to before Eve.

Duncan had just finished cleaning out a horse stall when his cell rang. He recognized the number. Did they have a meeting he had forgotten about? Possibly. His mind was on the woman he wanted in his bed on a permanent basis, and not work for a change.

"Amber, what can I do for you?"

"Duncan, he took her," Amber said, the fear palpable in her voice.

"Who did?" he asked. But he knew. The bastard had found her.

"Trevor Cleveland."

"When?" he chewed out.

"About ten minutes ago," Amber explained.

"I'm on my way. Just need to make a stop at home first. Call the sheriff."

"Grace already did. Hurry."

"Give me ten minutes. Fifteen, tops." He hung up, then called Eli.

"Dude, I swear I didn't—"

"Shut the fuck up, and listen. Eve's been kidnapped by that Trevor guy. I need you and Matt to meet me at Emmett's cabin. Bring your gear. Understood, soldier?"

"Got it, Lieutenant."

"Oh, and Eli, don't waste time. Be there in ten minutes," he snapped as he hung up, already rushing toward his vehicle. He noticed Maverick on the phone, his face hard and blazing with anger.

All the women had been getting together at Grace and Emmett's house. That bastard had threatened all their women. The fucker would be lucky if he survived until morning.

On the drive to his house, at speeds that were close to hyper speed and about as unsafe as one could drive on the winter mountain roads, Duncan worried about Eve. Jesus, he prayed she was still alive, and hadn't been hurt too badly.

At his cabin, he rushed inside and went to his gun cabinet. He might no longer be in the military, but he had lived for too long with a rifle in his hands to go without. He grabbed his rifle and a few clips that were packed already. He grabbed his shotgun, bowie knife, and began outfitting himself like he had every day for twelve years. He shoved extra ammo and a first aid kit into a small duffle bag. On his way out the door, he snatched one of the cozy blankets off the back of the couch.

Who knew what kind of shape he would find her in?

Eve had little bird bones, and was always cold. The errant thought that he might never see her again almost took his feet out from under him.

Like hell.

They hadn't had enough time together. He hadn't been gentle enough with her.

Forcing himself to move, he tossed everything in the passenger seat and sped off. Emmett and Grace's cabin was back a ways. When he pulled up, he had to park on the side of the road due to all the trucks and police vehicles lining the drive. The sheriff and his deputies were there already, which was good. They needed everyone they could find to search for her.

Duncan headed straight into the fray, located Amber, and said, "What happened?"

"He came in. Waved a gun around at everyone. Like he was going to shoot all of us," Amber said, her expression filled with shock.

"But Eve was so brave. She stood between us, went with him to save us," Morgan said with tears in her eyes.

Sampson pressed his face against Duncan's thigh. He scratched the pup's head. "I need to know which way they went. And then I'm heading out to find her."

"We're going to take a canvas approach. He couldn't have gotten far. I've got my deputies at the entrance to the ranch. If he passes through there, we'll get him," the sheriff stated, giving Duncan a once over, clocking all the firepower on his person like he approved.

That was a plus in their favor: Trevor couldn't leave the ranch. That was something. But they had a lot of territory to cover. And the ranch backed up to a national forest, where there was plenty of space to hide.

Matt and Eli strode in, decked out in the same fashion as Duncan. He nodded at them, then said to the sheriff, "Just tell me what direction he took out of here. Matt, Eli, and I will take that road."

It was Amber who said, "He went left out of the cabin driveway."

Bless her. She knew what the sheriff didn't: that with Matt and Eli at his back, Duncan was going to war.

"Then that's the direction the three of us will head. Sheriff, if you could come at them from the other direction? Taking a right out of here, then the left on the auxiliary road should have you meeting up with us somewhere in the middle."

"Where would you like us to look?" Maverick asked with his arm around Bianca.

Emmett was shoving shotgun shells into his coat pockets. "Bastard threatened my wife and son. I'm coming."

"Someone needs to stay behind, in case he circles back. Noah, why don't you stay here. Lincoln, you go with Mav and Emmett," Duncan said, thinking Lincoln would keep those two levelheaded as they hunted the bastard down.

"I'll call the other wranglers to be on the lookout as well," Mav stated like he had just thought of it, after a glance at his fiancée.

"I don't need to tell you all how dangerous this is. I'm officially deputizing all of you for this search. If Eve, as she is calling herself, is being harmed, don't hesitate to shoot the criminal," the sheriff said.

"What do you mean, calling herself Eve?" Duncan asked, stymied by the comment.

"I did some more digging after you brought this to my attention. I was going to tell you what I had found after Christmas, but the bastard upped my timeline. Her name isn't Eve Carruthers, it's Kate Jefferson. The bank that Trevor and his brother robbed belonged to her family," the Sheriff explained.

Duncan rocked back on his heels. She'd lied about her name. He'd thought they were much further than that when it came to trust. He had to shelve the knee-jerk betrayal he felt. Her life was in danger. Once he got her back, and assured himself that she was hale and hearty, he would give her the spanking of her life. "It doesn't matter what her name is, we need to find her. Who knows how much this guy has been terrorizing her the past year?"

"Everyone stay in contact. If you find them, let the rest of the group know your location. Let's move," the sheriff directed.

Duncan nodded at Amber as he left the cabin. Matt and Eli fell in line behind him, not saying anything until they were in his truck. Sampson jumped up in the back. Duncan peeled off before seatbelts were fastened.

"When we get to her, I want you to leave him to me. Got it?" Duncan snarled.

"We leaving him alive, boss?" Eli asked.

"What do you think?"

Matt snorted. "That dude was a walking dead man the moment he took what belongs to Duncan. Not to worry, we've got your back."

"Appreciate it." They weren't wrong. The only way Trevor Cleveland was leaving the ranch was in a body bag. And if Eve—or Kate, or whatever her damn name was—was injured or... dead... heaven help the man, because he would discover what hell really was.

he day had taken on a surreal bent. When Eve had woken up in Duncan's arms this morning, she hadn't thought that today would be the day she died. She shivered in the truck and watched her captor as he drove.

"I got you this time, didn't I, bitch?" he said gleefully, much like a kid after winning his favorite videogame.

"You did. How did you find me?" She had to keep him talking, it would distract him enough that she could plan. She paid attention to landmarks as they passed. If she had a chance to escape, however remote, she would take it. She wasn't going to lie down and give up just because her chances of making it out alive were slim.

He laughed with such arrogance, it made her cringe. "I told you the last time that I would always find you."

"Yeah, but how? I travelled off grid for a month."

"The dude making your IDs owed me a favor. I knew what name to look for to track you to this location."

"But I don't have credit cards or a bank account in

that name. My phone is a pay by month burner I paid cash for, so it doesn't make sense," she said as an idea began to form in her mind. It would be risky as hell. But it might be her one shot at escaping him.

She didn't have to worry about him returning to Grace's house. By now, Grace would have called her husband, and maybe even the police. They would be safe.

Trevor wouldn't expect her to strike out at him. The gun rested in his lap. Every once in a while, he stroked the handle, like he was dreaming about using it on her.

She wouldn't try to reach for it. But over these past few weeks, Duncan had taught her enough different techniques to defend herself. It was time to take what she had learned and use it. She would have to move fast. After she struck once, she wouldn't get more than a single chance to escape.

"Your name got a hit through the police department in town. I figured I would check it out. Been here a few days, getting the lay of the land." He chuckled. "Do you think I don't have contacts everywhere that owe me, bitch?"

She sucked in a breath. He had a contact in law enforcement. No wonder he always found her. It didn't surprise her about the guy making the fake IDs owing him a favor. "No. I knew you would find me eventually. Why don't you just kill me and get it over with?"

She was so tired of the cat and mouse game they had been playing, she wanted it done, one way or the other. She was done with running, with living in fear and looking over her shoulder.

"Because I've been thinking I want a taste of what my

brother enjoyed so much first, and then I'll kill you." He leered. His slimy gaze made her skin crawl.

Raped, then murdered in cold blood.

Fuck, she wasn't even going to be given a swift, painless end. She knew where they were on the road, what part of the ranch. If she could make it into the trees, she might stand a chance. Because while she was scared of going on the offense, she was petrified of what would happen if she didn't.

Knowing that it was now or never, with all her might, she swung at him with her bound hands, clocking him in the jaw, then grabbed the steering wheel, jerking the truck toward a tree on the roadside. At the speed he was going, the truck skidded off the road, bumped over uneven ground, and slammed into the tree.

The airbags deployed, knocking her head back against the seat. But she was already scrambling, unbuckling her seat belt. She flung her door open and rolled out before he could grab her.

"Get back here, you fucking bitch. I will end you."

She scraped her knee against the frozen tundra. Blood poured from the wound. She crawled to her feet, and ran, heading for the tree line to use for cover. She moved her legs even with her knee throbbing in pain.

If she stopped, or slowed down, he would catch her, and she would die.

Her head was viciously yanked back. She screamed, hoping against hope that people were out looking for her and would hear it.

He pressed the butt of the gun cruelly into her

temple. "Settle the fuck down, or I will end you right here."

"Do it. Just get it over with!" she yelled.

"Not until I've had my fun first. You owe me for all the shit you've caused me." Grabbing her bound wrists, he dragged her with him. "We go on foot now."

"Fuck you!" She spat in his face. "I don't owe you anything, you piece of shit."

The backhand snapped her head back. Pain erupted in her skull behind her eyes. And then she stumbled after him. He was heading higher up, toward some of the guest cabins.

She made it a point to be clumsy as she walked, marking their path as they went. Duncan could track her movements if he found the truck. She knew he could.

At the thought of Duncan, she almost lost it.

Cold seeped through her thermals until she was icy to the bone. As her teeth chattered, she wondered how fast hyperthermia would set in. She forgot what it was like to be warm as Trevor forced her to march behind him.

White snowflakes began to dance in the air around them. She looked up, and blanched. A storm was coming, picking up pace. It would cover her tracks before long.

Without those tracks, there was no hope that anyone, not even Duncan, would find her.

26

*W*ith Eve in the back of his mind, Duncan drove, scanning the road, looking in the driveways of the cabins they passed. Was she okay? Was she scared? She had to know that he would come for her. He just needed her to hold on.

"He couldn't have gone far," Matt said as they searched.

"Depends on how long the fucker has been in the area. He knew where to find her today," Eli commented.

"Probably followed her and planned his attack from there," Matt added, double checking the clip in his Glock.

"Doesn't matter how he found her. All that matters is where he is going with her and how much of a head start he has on us," Duncan snarled, his body vibrating with the need to do violence.

He didn't say that she had to be so frightened. When he got his hands on that asshole, he was a dead man.

"Boss, on your six!" Eli shouted.

He glanced where Eli pointed, and sucked in a breath. The truck had plowed into a tree. Skidding to a halt, he bolted from the truck with Sampson on his heels. On the passenger side, he spied the blood on the ground. He fought against his overwhelming fear for her.

Oh, baby. Hang on just a little longer for me.

"He's on foot. Matt, radio in our position. You two follow behind Sampson and me." Duncan didn't wait for them to protest or tell him to wait for the others. Time was of the essence.

He found the tracks within minutes. The fucker was getting sloppy. There was blood in the snow.

And from the way the tracks appeared, it looked like she was injured. Duncan and Sampson followed those footsteps swiftly, climbing along the tree line up into the higher elevations. He felt moisture on his cheek, touched it, and then glanced skyward.

Fuck me.

He whistled for Sampson, and heard Eli and Matt coming up behind him almost silently. A sharp, female scream pierced the air.

Duncan didn't think. He raced in the direction of her scream.

———

EVE HAD NEVER BEEN SO cold in her life. Her teeth chattered loudly as she trudged behind Trevor, hating him and his brother with a vengeance. She wanted it done. She didn't have any more in her to keep fighting.

Someone would come, but with the snow falling at a faster rate, she knew they wouldn't get to her in time.

She decided to push the envelope. If she was going to die, it was going to be on her terms. And not with Trevor coldly raping her before he killed her. She would rather be done with it now, consequences be damned.

"How did Silas die?" she asked, stumbling and sliding in the snow behind Trevor, determined to make this forced march as difficult as possible on him.

"Another prisoner knifed him in the yard. Gutted him. He bled out before we could get help. Why?" he snapped.

"I'm glad he died like that. Must have been painful. And he must have known he was going to die. It's pretty sweet justice."

The balled fist flew into her cheek with stunning force. Pain ricocheted through her body, and she wondered for a moment if he'd broken her jaw as she crumpled to the ground. He kicked her after she fell.

She screamed. She couldn't help it. The pain was too great, too overpowering for her to hold back.

Before he could kick her a second time, she curled into a ball, trying to protect herself.

"Get up," he ordered.

She moaned at the pain, ignoring his command.

He gripped her hair and screamed in her face, "I told you to get up!"

"Fuck you."

"Fine. You want to get down to business? Let's do it right here. It will be quicker than I would have liked but so be it."

Trevor descended upon her. She fought his hold, kicking out as he dragged her legs down and came down on top of her. With her bound hands, she pushed at his face and chest as he smacked her.

He reached up his hand to strike her again.

Out of nowhere, a big black ball of fur clamped its huge mouth over his hand and bit down with enough force, Trevor shouted in pain.

Eve recognized the marking on his snout. Sampson.

That must mean Duncan wasn't far behind. With hope surging in her chest, while Trevor was distracted by Sampson attempting to rip his hand off, she kneed him right in the balls, just like Duncan had taught her.

Trevor issued a strangled sound, brought the gun up, and fired. Sampson whimpered and staggered to the ground.

No. No, no, no, no.

"Sampson!" she cried. *Please be okay*.

"Drop the fucking gun, Trevor," Duncan's voice boomed.

Eve crawled up to her knees, desperate for a glimpse of his face, and needing to see if Sampson was alive. But it was the wrong move. Trevor pointed the gun directly at her temple. "Seems we're at an impasse. If you try to shoot me, she's dead."

"You'll meet your maker shortly after, if that happens. And where you're going—"

A shot rang out. Blood bloomed on Trevor's chest. He glanced down in shock, like he was surprised someone had gotten the upper hand.

And then he toppled over beside Eve, the light in his eye extinguished.

"Sampson!" she screamed, crawling over the ground to the pup.

Sampson looked up at her, panting, blood pouring from his back leg. She started to undo the buttons on her shirt. They needed to stop his bleeding.

But Duncan was there, cupping her face in his hands. "Honey, where are you hurt?"

"Don't worry about me. Sampson needs—"

"We'll get him taken care of," he said as Matt and Eli rushed onto the scene.

"I've got him. Will patch him up and then we can get him to the vet. You take care of her," Matt said, already going to work on Sampson.

"Sorry it took me so long," Eli said. "Fucker kept moving around on me."

"You did good. I only regret that I wasn't the one to do it. May he rot in fucking hell." Duncan turned back to her. "Come on. Matt will get Sampson taken care of, there's no one I trust more to see to him."

Until this point, she'd held the tears back, not really believing that she was safe, that it was over. But now she couldn't stop them as they slid down her cheeks. Duncan shouldered his rifle and scooped her up in his arms. She burrowed her face in his chest as he carried her toward freedom.

She would no longer have to keep looking over her shoulder. She didn't have to run any longer. The future that had once seemed bleak was now filled with an abundance of hope.

27

By the time they reached the road, police vehicles and trucks Kate didn't recognize were clogging it up. Faces scanned them as they emerged from the woods.

"We've got an ambulance on the way," the sheriff stated, looking her over before glancing at Duncan.

"Good. We need to take her to the hospital, and then Sampson to the emergency vet. Fucker shot him," Duncan explained.

"And Cleveland?" the Sheriff asked with an impassive, unreadable expression.

"Dead. There was no way around it," Duncan stated, and a look passed between the two men.

The sheriff absorbed the news with a slight nod. "Where? My men and I can deal with it from here."

"I'll take you, Sheriff. I was the one who shot him. Follow me," Eli said after rejoining the group.

Matt approached with Sampson in his arms just as the ambulance arrived. Safe, Kate floated in and out, like she was there... but not. She was likely in shock after the day's events, and who could blame her?

"Ma'am, we're going to get you on a stretcher now. What's your name, hon?"

She tried to avoid having to give a legal name. She murmured, "Uh—"

"Kate Jefferson," Duncan stated.

She glanced up at him. His look spoke volumes. He knew that she had lied about her name but didn't hate her for it. She placed her hand on his cheek. There was so much she wanted—no, needed—to say to him. Warm understanding entered his eyes as he gripped her hand and placed a kiss in the palm. "I know, honey. Let's get you fixed up first."

She was loaded onto the stretcher, and they began taking her vitals. Matt walked over with Sampson in his arms.

"I don't know if there's room for the dog," the EMT stated, glancing at the injured pup.

"Put him on the stretcher with me. He's a hero. My hero. One of them," she said, looking up at Duncan with her heart in her eyes. She was free because of him.

Matt brought Sampson over and laid him down gently beside her. Sampson put his head on her belly. She stroked his head. "You're such a good boy, Sampson. I'm going to bake you all the treats in the world."

Sampson licked her hand. God, she loved them both so much, she thought as they were loaded into the waiting ambulance. Duncan climbed in the back with her. And she knew that, no matter what, everything would work out. It had to. They had come too far for it not to.

———

It was hours before Kate was given a mostly clean bill of health with a few cuts, scrapes and bruises. Sampson made it through surgery, and was spending the night recovering in the emergency vet clinic before Duncan would bring him home tomorrow.

He took her straight to his house, not even asking if she wanted to go home.

But then, it had been a full afternoon with plenty of visitors. Grace and Emmett stopped by the hospital with little Jamie. Maverick and Bianca stopped by with flowers. Morgan, Noah, and their boys brought chocolate chip cookies. Amber, Lincoln, Matt, Eli, Noelle, Mrs. Gregory, even Jessica and Mike—everyone came to check on her. Amber told Kate she was not to return to work until after the first of the year, and then they would talk more about the bakery.

But it was the man she had barely been able to speak two words to alone all evening whom she worried about most.

When she tried to climb down out of his truck under her own steam, he glared. "Put your arms around my neck, honey. No arguments."

Because it hurt to move, even with the mild painkillers they had given her, she complied, too tired to argue with him.

Besides, she loved the feel of his arms around her, especially when at one point today, she hadn't known whether she would ever feel them again. Inside the cabin, she looked around. While they had been at the hospital, their friends had been busy little bees. There were more flowers—everywhere, it seemed.

"The fridge is full of meals that Mrs. Gregory made for us. That way, you don't have to worry about cooking for the next few days and can rest and heal." He carried her over to the sofa and sat with her in his arms.

"Duncan, I... I'm sorry. That I didn't tell you my real name. I wanted to, so much."

"I get why you didn't. His eye—you did that, didn't you?"

She nodded. "Yeah. He attacked me in the kitchen of my parents' house. My house, really. I don't know if it's legally still mine or not. I used my keys and punched him in the eye. That was the side effect. And then I ran. I assumed a new alias every time he found me. I didn't want to lie to people, but I was—"

He stroked a comforting hand up and down her back. "Terrified. And with good reason. You have nothing to be sorry for. I'm not mad, not after seeing what he did to you and knowing how much worse it could have been. And if I hadn't gotten there in time—"

She put her fingers over his mouth. "But you did. Don't you get it? It's because of you that I had the courage to make him run into that tree and try to get away."

At her confession, he lowered his forehead to hers and whispered, "Jesus. I'm so sorry I wasn't faster."

She cupped his cheek. "I'm trying to get this out. I need to say this. I know we've not been together that long, and this might seem rather sudden. But a life and death experience really changes your perception and makes time seem rather meaningless... what I'm trying to say—"

"I love you too, Eve or Kate, or whatever name you want to go by."

Tears slipped down her face. "Duncan, I do love you, more than you can possibly imagine."

"I can imagine pretty much." He wiggled his brows and made her chuckle.

"You're incorrigible. But it's just one of the many things I adore about you."

He caressed his palm down her back. "You know, when I woke up this morning, I had every intention of asking you to move in with me."

"You did?" she gasped.

"Was going to."

"You're not anymore?" She tried not to let her disappointment show, because she would love to live with him.

Duncan pegged her with an intense stare. "No. It's not enough for me, not after I came so close to losing you today. I think you're just going to have to marry me."

"Oh. I am, huh?" Joy burst in a cacophony inside her chest as happiness spilled forth. This man was everything to her. He'd helped her find her confidence, and given her a chance at a new life.

"Yep. And after hearing about your heroics, protecting everyone at Emmett and Grace's earlier today, I'm going to want some kids too. Half a dozen should just about do it, I'm thinking."

"Half a dozen? You're crazy. I don't even know how we would manage that."

"Crazy about you, and we'll figure it out as we go."

He shrugged like it would be no big deal to have that many.

"So we're doing this? We're getting married? For real?" she asked breathlessly, almost too afraid to hope.

"Yep. I even picked out a ring."

She sputtered, "You... When?"

"After that first night in the tent. I thought I was nuts when I did it, but now I can see that I knew even then what you meant to me. It just took my brain a little longer to catch up."

"That long, huh? I knew the first time you kissed me. Pissed me off, too. I wasn't supposed to get involved with anyone. Emotional ties would make it too hard to run again. But I couldn't seem to help myself where you were concerned," she admitted.

He pressed his mouth to hers in a soul-stirring, gentle kiss. "I can't, either—help myself, that is. But then, you already know that."

"You know, there's going to be legal stuff I have to deal with. I might even have to head back to Georgia to settle things," she warned him, wanting full disclosure with no more secrets between them.

"We'll deal with it together. That's how we're strongest. And to be honest, after today, I'm not letting you out of my sight for a while."

"I never thanked you, you know, for saving my life."

"Honey, I will always come for you, no matter what. No thanks are necessary... although there are ways you could thank me. We could start our Christmas celebration a little early." He wiggled his brows suggestively, making her laugh. And then he kissed her, holding her tight, showing her that she was more loved than she had ever known was possible.

As the clock struck twelve, ushering in Christmas, she couldn't help but be thankful for the greatest gift she had ever received: the love of her valiant cowboy. They wouldn't always agree on everything, it wasn't how they were built.

But a life loving Duncan was more than she had ever thought possible. And she didn't want to miss a thing.

HOW TO ROPE A SAVAGE COWBOY
SILVER SPRINGS RANCH SERIES, BOOK 6

Lincoln is floundering. He did something undeniably stupid. On an evening out with his best buddies in Vegas, he hooked up with a smoking hot female for a torrid, all night escapade. It was one of the most carnal experiences of his life, and one he wouldn't be averse to repeating.

Under most circumstances, a one-night stand wouldn't be an issue. Except, the woman is his boss and his best friend's sister. If his buddy discovers their tryst, Lincoln is a dead man. Utter disaster. And yet, there was something about that night that makes him want to risk life and limb to hold her, experience her scorchingly addictive surrender again.

As if that isn't bad enough, after they return home, her ex-boyfriend appears in a bid to win her back, unleashing the territorial beast inside Lincoln. She belongs to him, not some city slicker in a suit.

He plans to prove to her that she belongs in his bed. That he's the only one who should be gifted with her seductive surrender.

Now he's navigating wooing his boss, and falling for her. Can he convince Amber to take a chance on him for more than one night?

Get it now!

MIDNIGHT MASQUERADE
DUNGEON SINGLES NIGHT SERIES, BOOK 1

Sophia is in trouble. Again.

Maybe it's the masks. Maybe she needs to feel something other than regret.

Whatever the reason, she is either daring... or foolish... when she trades places with another submissive, and ends up spending the night in her mysterious boss's bed.

He doesn't recognize her, but now she's had him, she knows one taste of his dark love will never be enough.

Gabriel Ryan has one firm rule: don't sleep with employees.

Even though he's infuriated beyond measure to discover Sophia in his bed after a night of mind-blowing pleasure, she is now in his blood. He craves her. Needs her. Yearns for her surrender.

But she is forbidden. He will break her with his dark desires.

When Sophia's dangerous past waltzes into his club, Gabriel must protect her. He must claim her. And break every single one of his rules to keep her safe.

Head to Eternal Eros! Get it now!

ALSO BY ANYA SUMMERS

Dungeon Singles Night Series

Midnight Masquerade

Midnight Mystique

Midsummer Night's Dream

Midnight Renegade

Midnight Rendezvous

A Knight To Remember

Midnight Highlander

Silver Springs Ranch Series

How To Rope A Wild Cowboy

How To Rope A Rich Cowboy

How To Rope A Rough Cowboy

How To Rope A Loyal Cowboy

How To Rope A Valiant Cowboy

How To Rope A Savage Cowboy

The Manor Series

The Man In The Mask

Torn In Two

Redeemed By Love

Box Sets

Dungeon Singles Night Collection Part 1

How To Rope A Cowboy Box Set

The Man In The Mask: The Complete Manor Series
Collection

ABOUT ANYA

Born in St. Louis, Missouri, Anya grew up listening to Cardinals baseball and reading anything she could get her hands on. She remembers her mother saying if only she would read the right type of books instead binging her way through the romance aisles at the bookstore, she'd have been a doctor. While Anya never did get that doctorate, she graduated cum laude from the University of Missouri-St. Louis with an M.A. in History.

Anya is a bestselling and award-winning author published in multiple fiction genres. She also writes urban fantasy, paranormal romance, and contemporary romance under the name Maggie Mae Gallagher. A total geek at her core, when she is not writing, she adores attending the latest comic con or spending time with her family. She currently lives in the Midwest with her two furry felines.

www.anyasummers.com
anya@anyasummers.com

Join Anya's mailing list to be the first to be notified of new releases, free books, exclusive content, special prizes and author giveaways!
https://anyasummers.com/newsletter/

Follow Anya on social media!

Facebook: facebook.com/AnyaSummersAuthor

Twitter: twitter.com/anyabsummers

Instagram: instagram.com/anyasummersauthor

Goodreads: goodreads.com/author/show/
15183606.Anya_Summers

BookBub: bookbub.com/authors/anya-summers